The Maid and the Cook

by Eris Adderly

This book is a work of fiction. Names, characters, places, and incidents either are products of the author's imagination or are used fictitiously. Any resemblance to actual persons, living or dead, events, or locales is entirely coincidental.

THE MAID AND THE COOK

First eBook Edition: December 2015
Kindle Edition

Cover Design by Eris Adderly.

Acknowledgements

Thank you to all the people who appreciate a story that wasn't about the lords and ladies, kings or princesses, with their perfectly chiselled jaws and flawless silky skin, and wealth and education and all of life's advantages. Regular, flawed people like us need love and sexy times, too. For his sharp editing eye, Mr Jim, you are the best. For beta-reading the original version, Jodie, you know I love you.

Contents

Chapter 1

Honey and Bone

"Man cannot spend all his time doing evil, and even in the company of pirates there must be some sweet moments on their sinister ship when you feel as if you were aboard a pleasure yacht."

– Honoré de Balzac, *The Human Comedy*

"It is a mistake to think you can solve any major problems just with potatoes."

– Douglas Adams, *Life, the Universe and Everything*

Bristol, England, 1716

"Brigit, if you'll return to our room, please, to wait for our things? I'll join you again as soon as I've spoken with the captain."

"As you wish, Ma'am." She moved to obey Mrs Collingwood's words, though her reluctance to return to the tiny cabin below decks must have showed on her pitted face. Brigit wasn't sure whether the widow speaking with the captain alone was such a good idea.

The steps to the lower deck marched away under her feet again as she made her way back to the dark little room. She kept her eyes averted from the considering glances she received from passing sailors as she went, but what Brigit most hoped to avoid seeing was any more of that greasy surgeon.

She and her employer, the Widow Collingwood of Bristol, had been shown their cabin by an oily lizard of a man claiming to be the surgeon aboard *The Mourning Dove*. Brigit had grown an immediate dislike for the man, though he'd only said a handful of words in her presence, and she was quite relieved to see the back of him once he'd left her and the widow in their cabin.

The cabin, she thought, slipping back through its narrow door again, was close and dark, and made the backs of her hands itch just sitting in it. She'd never been on a journey by sea of this length, and the weak glow of an oil lamp fastened to the outer wall did nothing to reassure her it would be a pleasant trip. Neither did the widow's company.

They'd be at least six weeks at sea before making port in Boston, and the prim daughter of one Richard Symes—House of Commons, if you please—was from a world so far removed from Brigit's own she had no idea how to begin to interact with the woman, despite her stuffy attempts at conversation.

The widow had tried to engage her in light chatter, but much of what she'd said had gone over Brigit's head. The maid from Cork suspected the stiff-backed blonde, several years her senior, could stand to have her demeanour improved by a bit more time with her legs in the air instead of with her head in a book. Of course, thoughts of that nature could never be uttered aloud. She'd have been standing in Bristol port right now, unemployed, if she'd said each cheeky thought that came to mind.

Brigit hoisted herself up onto the slim bunk that lined one side of the cabin and leaned back against the wall behind, her legs dangling at the knee over the edge. Closing her eyes, she tried to imagine which might be worse: more than a month at sea, stuck with the widow in this dark cubby hole, where it appeared she'd have to sleep on the bare floor, or remaining at home, with her five younger siblings, an abundance of noise and complaints, and a frequent lack of both meals and peace.

She was still undecided on the matter as she began to doze.

A sharp rap at the door was all the warning Brigit had to start her awake before a man's head popped into the cabin. A blond sailor about her same age with a narrow beak of a nose aimed a question at her, but she was still rubbing sleep out of bleary eyes.

"I'm sorry?" she said, squinting at him, readjusting to the dim light.

"I said, you're the lady's maid, yes?"

"I am."

"Cap'n wants to see you."

"What for?" she asked, still confused as she straightened her skirts and stood. Where was the widow?

"Didn't say. Only told me to fetch you." He stood in a casual lean against the doorframe as if this were the most normal request in the world, and when she didn't move he prompted her with a loose gesture of his hand. "Come on, then."

He didn't seem to have any intention of leaving without her.

She pushed a breath out through her nose and screwed up her lips as she made to follow and, seeing her doing as he asked, the young sailor turned to go.

Why would the captain need to see her? A lady's maid? What had happened when he'd 'had a word' with the widow? In all likelihood the woman sliced him with that sharp tongue of hers and now they would both be in hot water. Brigit sighed in resignation as she picked her way along behind the crew member leading her. There was no way this was heading for anything pleasant.

The bright daylight made her eyes water as soon as they stepped back up onto the main deck, and it took a round of blinking to clear them. Her quick glances around told her they were already well out to sea. There was no sign of land in any direction.

The blond man's smart steps carried them aft to a doorway leading below again. A shorter set of steps than the first she'd descended brought her and the sailor into a large room dominated by a long table at its centre.

Chairs surrounded the heavy table on both sides and at one end. The cabin felt as though it might be meant for meetings or perhaps formal meals, but Brigit couldn't be sure; she'd never seen this part of a ship before today.

The man who'd exchanged blunt words with the widow occupied the seat at the head of the table.

Mrs Collingwood was nowhere in sight.

The sailor cleared his throat. "Captain," he said. "The lady's maid."

After a final bit of scratching with a quill on the leaf of paper before him, the captain raised his head to acknowledge their presence.

"Thank you, Hawke." He nodded at the man standing just behind her now. "And did you tell Mr Bone I needed to speak with him as well?"

"Aye, Sir. I went to him first; let him have more time to make his way down."

"Smart choice, Hawke. That will be all."

Giving a quick nod at his dismissal, the sailor made his way back up into the blinding sunlight.

Brigit stood there alone with this captain, in his fine coat and hat. She didn't care for it.

He slid the paper off to the side and rested his hands on the table, lacing his fingers together. Dark eyes looked up at her. Arrogance and breeding sang from the cut of his jaw and the arch of his brows. She fought an urge to smirk.

Of course his kind would be an officer. They all felt the need to order others about, didn't they?

"You are Mrs Collingwood's maid, Mrs ...?"

These people and their silly formalities. He knows I'm her maid.

"Brigit." She gave her name as he asked, trying not to be cheeky and make trouble.

"Brigit with no last name?"

She sighed to herself. "O'Creagh."

"I see," he said, the lightest dusting of judgement on his tone as he noted her accent. Brigit liked him even less. "Well, Mrs O'Creagh, it seems there's been a bit of a misunderstanding."

Oh dear Lord. What did that woman do?

She waited for him to speak again, fiddling with the folds of her apron as she stood there.

"It is my understanding the two of you were meant to board and sail on *The Mourning Dove?*" he asked, head cocked slightly and brow raised. She suspected he already knew the answer to his own question.

"That's correct, Captain." She squirmed in place, trying to put herself on her best behaviour.

"Well, Mrs O'Creagh, I'm afraid that's the trouble. *The Mourning Dove* is likely still at port. You've been seen aboard *The Devil's Luck* instead, and unfortunately I've no intention of turning about. I do apologise, but it looks as though you'll be with us for a time."

"*The Devil's Luck!*" Brigit heard little after the infamous name. "*The Devil's Luck* is a bloody pirate ship! Then that would make you ..." She began to step backwards, the reality of her surroundings, and just who this man was, landing on her.

"Yes, yes, Black Edmund, I see the name precedes me." He waved her off in irritation. "And I'll have you mind your tone, Mrs O'Creagh. I've tolerance for exactly one woman with a tart mouth today, and your former employer's already used that up."

"My *former* employer?" she said, incredulous, not sure whether to be incensed or terrified. Brigit held no particular love for the woman, but neither did she want to be alone on a ship full of criminals. "What has happened to Mrs Collingwood?"

"Captain, ye wanted to see me?" The deep boom of a male voice behind her accompanied several wooden thumps, announcing the arrival of another crew member, and cutting off Brigit's frantic line of question.

She turned to the source of the interruption and was faced with perhaps the largest bear of a man she'd ever seen. At least a head taller than her and easily twice as wide, his shadow darkened the room for a moment as his enormous frame filled the door.

As he made his way into the room, she discovered the source of the thumping: his left leg was missing below the knee. In its place was a dark wooden peg. Life on a ship was far from safe.

Especially this *ship. The Devil's Luck. How on earth had they ...?*

"Yes, Mr Bone." The captain ignored Brigit for his new visitor. "You've had no help in your galley since we lost Mr James, is that correct?"

"Aye, Sir."

"Then congratulations are in order, Bone. Mrs O'Creagh here will take over, starting today. I trust you know your way around a kitchen, then?" He aimed the last bit at her.

"If you *please*, Captain," she said, straining to check her temper at the complete lack of an explanation for this impossible turn of events, "what has happened to Mrs Collingwood?"

The man sighed, tossing his hat onto the long table, leaning back in his chair, annoyance with the entire situation plain on his face. "She's no longer in need of your services, Mrs O'Creagh. Be thankful I've set you to work for Mr Bone in the galley instead of allowing you to roam free among the crew." He arched a meaningful brow her way, and she took his import.

Pirates.

Another thought occurred to her.

"You haven't..." She stammered, growing more nervous by the moment. "You haven't ... *killed* her? Have you?"

"Of course not!" he said, indignant as he sat up straight again. "What do you take me for?"

Brigit was *not* going to answer that question, but her mind flung down answers all the same.

A pirate. A cutthroat. A bloody thief, a murderer.

She glanced back towards the towering Mr Bone and found him eyeing her, a heavy hand stroking along the twin plaits of a dark red beard that hung half-way down his chest. The big man's blue eyes considered her from beneath ginger brows and a shaven skull. Brigit tried to make herself small.

"Mrs O'Creagh," the captain said, sounding tired, "it's the galley or be unattended on my ship. Which is it?"

Brigit swallowed. She'd dealt with crude enough men before, but none such as these. How might she know which would be the least horrible choice?

How is this happening at all?

"The galley then." She settled for what seemed the lesser of two evils, resentful.

"Very well. Mr Bone—"

"Captain, wait!" she said, likely overstepping her bounds once again. "I don't understand! How is it we were seen aboard *your* ship and not *The Mourning Dove?* Your surgeon said—"

"My *surgeon*," he said with a sneer. "I assure you, Mrs O'Creagh, you'd prefer not to know the how and why of it."

"Try me," she said, folding her arms, mildly defiant again. She would be the judge of what she might want to know.

Careful, Brigit, you've already annoyed him once.

Her tiny challenge for information earned her a mild snort of amusement from Bone.

"I see you won't leave well enough alone then," the captain said. "Do remember it was *you* who insisted."

A right bastard, this one is.

"It seems," he continued, "that my surgeon wanted your Mrs Collingwood aboard for a bit of sport, and so he led her to believe she was safely boarding *The Mourning Dove*, when in fact she—and you—were not."

"A bit of *sport?* He didn't …" Brigit's stomach dropped once she took the captain's meaning. That surgeon had been … sickening.

"I see that you follow. Be grateful you were discovered right away. And that I won't be handing you back to him."

She pressed her lips together. This man likely deserved whatever tongue-lashing he'd received from the widow, and Brigit disliked the woman a trifle less now for it.

Wherever she is.

"Questions, Bone?" The captain turned his attention back to the other man.

"None, Captain," he said, shifting his weight onto his good leg. He then appeared to think better on it, though. "Well … maybe. Where should I have her sleep?"

The captain gave his cook a half-smirk as he took his quill up again. "I'm sure you'll figure something out, Mr Bone."

Brigit caught the tall man's eyes at that comment. Where *would* she sleep? What about the cabin that—

Oh.

That had been the surgeon's cabin, she realised, and not a cabin set aside for her and the widow. This wasn't *The Mourning Dove*, after all. No, she was most certain she didn't want to go back *there* to sleep. Not any more.

Bone inclined his head towards the captain, accepting his instructions, or lack thereof, and turned to Brigit with a shrug, shouldering his new charge as though it were every day Black Edmund assigned him young maids to help him with his duties.

"It looks like the galley for ye, then. Follow along." He turned to mount the steps again, not even looking back, already expecting her to do as asked. It appeared every man aboard this ship would be ordering her to come here and go there.

She squinted at the captain and gave him a final *harrumph* of distaste, though his eyes were back on whatever he'd been writing. There was nothing to be done for it. Brigit would have to deal with this cook.

For now, at least. They have to make port somewhere else eventually.

Turning on her heel, she stalked off after him.

Brigit caught up to the bald man without much effort, his wooden leg keeping him from too brisk a pace. He must have had a keen ear, because he heard her steps behind him without having to turn his head and see her fall in.

"Have ye spent much time on a ship, Mrs O'Creagh?"

"Not as long as this trip was expected to be," she said to the back of his head. "And just 'Brigit' will do."

The constant use by this crew, these pirates, of her family name was both unfamiliar and out of place. She hadn't been raised among the sort of social circles which held to that level of formality. Unlike her employer—her *former* employer, Brigit reminded herself—her family and their friends hadn't bothered awfully much about 'Mister' and 'Missus'. The titles didn't go well with the stockings that needed darning and the bare cupboards so common in her part of town.

And these rough men, sailors all, to persist in addressing her this way? It seemed a means of mocking her. She knew what she looked like.

The cook grunted at her request to be called by her first name, but continued his purposeful stroll along the deck.

He brought them to a set of stairs leading below and, with a surprising amount of skill for a man with a false leg, descended without a pause, calling to her over his shoulder: "Mind yer step on the way down."

Brigit took in a breath and hoisted her skirts several inches, steeling herself to follow this enormous man she'd barely met down into the bowels of the galleon.

The Devil's Luck. She shuddered to herself.

That inn back in Bristol seemed like a corner of paradise now.

The galley was darker and cooler than the open air of the main deck and again her eyes needed to adjust as she stepped down into it. She'd just managed to brace herself to cope with her new situation when the cook's casual warning became a tidy little prophecy.

Brigit put her foot wrong on one of the narrow steps and went tumbling headlong into the dim space below her.

John Bone turned back around just in time to hear a startled cry and what may have been a curse out of the young maid as she evaded his cautionary words and followed a turned ankle and loss of balance down into the galley, face first.

A swift step forward and thrust of his hands caught her up under her arms, and he spared her the rude introduction to the deck, hauling her upright once he had her in a sure grip.

Still off balance, her upper body fell against his, and she clutched at his shirt, his belt, to try to remain standing. He moved his hold out from under her arms and caught her about the waist, steadying her. As urgency faded, a new problem struck him.

A soft, feminine form stood crushed up against him. A healthy, freckled bosom rose and fell above tight stays as the maid caught her breath. Green eyes rolled up over his chest and neck, wide now as they met his own. She, too, saw the way her fall had pressed them together.

Some warm, sleeping thing turned over low in his gut then.

God, but it's been a long time, hasn't it John?

He cleared his throat.

"Are ye … alright? Mrs O'Creagh?"

The maid stared up at him, and he swore he could see her pulse at her throat.

"Brigit?" He corrected himself. It was what she'd asked to be called, wasn't it?

She wet her lips with an absent slip of pink tongue, and shifted her feet to better support herself, not once tearing her eyes from his.

"I think I'm … alright ... Mr Bone." The young woman tugged backwards in his arms, appearing to test whether he would release her.

He loosed his arms, as if in a trance, and let her step back.

What just happened here?

Shaking his mind back to attention, he turned into the dim interior of the room and pushed off into the instruction he'd planned as he'd first led her across the deck.

"Right. Well. This is the galley then." He began to move about the space, his unexpected new charge following. "This is the oven, and here is where we keep the pots …"

John Bone busied himself showing Brigit around, but all the while his thoughts danced and played elsewhere, the way *he* might have before he lost the leg. Glances at the younger woman—his best estimations gave him some twenty years over her—told him beneath the scars dusting her face there was a saucy grin, the likes of which made a man act the fool. He already found himself tempted to do so.

Ye know I like a calm sea, Blackburn. What storm have ye dropped on me here?

A man his age should know better.

Brigit tried to pay attention to what the cook was saying—something about pease, just now—but her mind kept fluttering back to her fall down the stairs. And into this pirate's arms.

She didn't suspect any devious intention from the man. The surprised grunt out of him when he caught her up told her he'd only meant to save her from a spill. It was when she recognised the way their bodies were crushed together, his massive arms circling her. That sudden flash of awareness in his blue eyes when she'd met them.

That was the look shared between two people when some external force reminds them one of them is a man and the other a woman, in the most basic, animal sense of the words. A male and female. Two bodies, pressed close and secluded. The maid from Cork flushed at the thought.

The man's nearly twice your age, girl!

He was, though, wasn't he? She noted the white beginning to thread into his beard at the edges, and the way the corners of his eyes crinkled as he explained the routines of the galley with a sprinkling of salty humour. Not a gawky youth at all like the few she'd let cover her in the odd barn or midnight hillside.

She was no innocent at twenty-three, but someone with a face like hers hadn't the luxury of the pick of the litter, as far as men were concerned. She'd taken what attention she could get, though it had most often been as no more than a convenient warm place, and not as the sort of beauty who inspired songs and poems.

Smallpox taking her as a girl had done no favours for

her appearance. But for a moment, she'd almost imagined he'd looked at her as though the awful reminders of her long-ago illness weren't riddled across her features. As though she were some comely lass at a country dance he wished to bounce on his knee.

"Well?" he said.

Brigit scattered her silly thoughts aside. He was gesturing at her with a potato in one hand and a small paring knife in the other. She blinked at him.

You haven't been paying attention at all! Try not to annoy a man the size of this one, will you?

"We'd best be on about it then," he said, and she thought he might be repeating something she'd missed, lost in thought as she'd been. "Takes a fair amount of time to prepare evening meal for a crew this size. Can ye handle the potatoes?"

She didn't know the proper way to respond, and so instead stepped forward and took the knife and potato from him. This was her place now, wasn't it? To work for this cook?

A glance back to the tall cutting block behind her showed the promise of a healthy share of work: a bulky sack holding the rest of the unpeeled potatoes leaned against its side. With a final considering eye for the imposing Mr Bone, she turned to her task.

From lady's maid to cook's mate in the span of hours, she mused. Where the widow was in all this, she had no idea and was, in all honesty, afraid to ask. She wondered which of the two of them had got the worst in this bargain. The widow, unlike Brigit, was something to look at. And this was a ship full of men who'd been at sea long enough to take what they wanted without asking.

Perhaps men like this cook?

Brigit blushed again when she thought she spied him casting an eye her way. Forcing her attention down to the knife in her hands, she set to work.

He'd only given her the peeling to do because it was a near endless task, and he preferred her to be standing in one place, and out of his way, for the time being. Potatoes were one of the foodstuffs, like water, that didn't keep long on a ship, and it was best to make use of them right away, before they spoiled.

That and he was already so accustomed to working alone. At least he was since they'd lost his last mate just over a year ago while relieving a packet of its cargo off the coast of Florida. A lead ball in the chest does much to impede the business of living.

He wasn't yet sure how to weave another set of hands into his routines again. There was an entire process to readying the galley for the evening meal, and he'd perfected his dance for one. Two in the kitchen would require time to sort out who was best suited to what all over again.

It would also require him to stop staring at the circle of this maid's waist, and the way her hips shifted as she moved her weight from one foot to the other, trying to spare her knees from a task that required her to stand in the same place for a length of time. Images of her bent at the middle over the edge of the cutting block, skirts up over her round bottom, did nothing to preserve the usual comfortable lull of his chores, either.

The last of the salt pork tumbled into the simmering stew pot and he wiped the grease from his hands with a rag. Turning back to his new responsibility, he folded his arms over his chest and leaned against the pantry doorframe, watching her work. The pile of peelings was growing off to one side of the block's surface under deft movements of her knife. Her head was bent to her task, exposing the line of her neck to the frank appraisal he felt waking up somewhere beneath his ribs.

John Bone hadn't felt this ready to jump out of his skin over a woman in years. He didn't lighten his purse with whoring nearly as often as most of the other, younger crew members did during shore leave. At their age, the entire wide world was a place to put their cocks, and they were all stallions looking for a mare. Experience showed him now, though, that a poxy wench most often wasn't worth the coin for the few minutes' rut. He was already missing part of one limb: the rest he'd like to keep intact, if it pleased the Lord.

The long braids of his beard slid under his fingers as he smoothed at them in the usual way he did when he thought. He fiddled with the tin charms he'd woven into the ends of the plaits, a bull on one and a rose on the other. His hands, he realised as he took in the sloping shoulders of the maid, wished to be busy elsewhere.

Even in his youth, he'd never been aggressive when it came to women: he preferred to suss out their interest and watch matters spring up in due course. This Brigit O'Creagh, however … Her name even tasted good rolling around in his mouth. Perhaps it was the husky giggles that bubbled up out of her at his rude attempts at humour. Or possibly the way her cheeks dimpled beneath the scars. That accent of hers wasn't hurting either. Cork, she'd told him, when he'd asked where her family was from.

Whatever it was about her, he'd felt it sinking into him while he'd been showing her about the galley, and the level of his boldness was rising to meet it. The near endless patience he was known for among the crew became a thing of unfamiliar frustration now. Perhaps, he thought, today he might press his advantage instead of waiting. He had size and years over her, and the galley was *his* personal fiefdom, after all, and not hers.

He wouldn't force anything, but maybe …

Maybe today, and with this young woman, he could find it in himself to be … persuasive.

"So how did ye end up in the service of this … Mrs Collingwood, is it?

Brigit turned to look over her shoulder at the first words she'd heard from the cook in a while, and saw him leaning near the door to the pantry he'd shown her. His weight was on his good leg, as she was coming to note it often was, and he had those massive arms folded across the front of him.

"My da' heard from one of his friends there was some gentleman in need of a maid for his daughter's travels," she said. Something about the cook's presence, some warmth perhaps, put her at ease, and she expanded: "He had me volunteered and signed on before sunset without even asking me. Said the family needed more coin and less mouths to feed."

"Ye mean ye'll see no purse at all for yer work?" He sounded incredulous, though his voice was still sedate. She laughed without turning back to look at him.

"Oh no, Mr Bone. My da' had that coin in hand before the ink was dry on the paper." She gave a rueful chuckle at the memory of the glimmer in her father's eye when the silver had been displayed that evening at the family's table. "Not that it matters now, I suppose. This captain of yours seems to have relieved me of my duties, at least to the widow."

"She's a widow, is she?"

The knife gleamed before disappearing under the surface of the next potato.

"So it seems, Mr Bone," she answered him, "but I think it's been for some time now. She doesn't wear weeds, and she never speaks of Mr Collingwood." Brigit was relaxing in the company of this man. She could almost forget what he was.

Pirate.

"Oh dear Lord," he said with a groan.

"What's that then? Is it a problem?" She turned her head again to see if she could read the meaning on his face, and saw that he'd levered himself away from the doorframe.

"Not for you, it won't be, lass." He made a low noise she thought might have been a laugh, and his eyes were elsewhere, mind on matters out of sight.

"For who then? The widow?" She went back to her peeling, adding another finished potato to the stack.

"Let us just say"—the thump of his wooden leg told her he was moving about the galley now as he collected his thoughts—"a man like Captain Blackburn finds a woman like that in his care? Well … It may be best if ye didn't know."

Brigit smirked as the knife made its next chalky bite. She imagined she likely *did* know. That poor woman. The widow looked as though she wouldn't know what to do with a man if he walked straight up to her and—

The cook was behind her.

Directly behind her.

Chest to her shoulders, belt to her waist, pressed against her all the way down. Her paring knife fell to the block with a dull clatter and she took a brisk breath in through her nose.

Closer he crowded her, until her belly came against the side of the block and she was trapped between him and it. Her heart thudded at a wild pace and her palms were flat on the cutting surface, her limbs too stunned to make a move.

The immense, warm upper body of a man curved in around her, and she saw heavy hands come to rest at the edge of the block on either side. Her arms, which on any normal day she considered plump, looked almost delicate alongside his. She swallowed and stared straight ahead at the galley's staircase.

You may have become too *familiar with this man, Brigit.*

"Did anyone tell ye to stop peeling, Mrs O'Creagh?" His voice was a deep, tumbling purr, just above her right ear. She'd asked him to use her first name instead, but the way he'd addressed her just now stirred up a hum of awareness between her thighs. Her knees wanted to buckle, but she managed to keep them locked.

At an utter loss for words, she flicked her gaze back down at the block and took up the knife once more, along with the half-skinned potato she'd dropped, and tried to focus again on her task. Bone didn't move.

How long will he stand here like this?

"So what will yer father do with this coin, now that he's hired ye out as a maid?" He spoke to her in quiet tones, but in a casual way that belied the heat of his body, the rustle of his shirt and breeches against her back.

"Well"—she cleared her throat, the knife moving its slowest yet—"I suppose the family will eat now."

"Mmm? Weren't they eating before?" His left hand came away from the block with his distracted question, and she felt a set of knuckles drag in a whisper down the back of her upper arm.

How could he expect her to keep working while he did this?

"Not as much as they'd like, I'm sure, Mr Bone." All of her willpower went into keeping her voice steady. Why it seemed so important to play along, to act as if nothing out of the ordinary was happening, was beyond her.

"And why is that?" His voice was so very low and dark with temptation now. The hand moved to her waist and settled there.

Yes, there was clearly a game afoot. And one she was certain this man would win in the end, but that didn't mean she couldn't be sporting. Brigit took a deep, slow breath and picked up a new potato.

"I'm the oldest of six by ten years, Mr Bone." She made her reply, trying her best to ignore him while she worked again with the knife. "Four brothers and one sister. My da' could hardly keep food in the cupboard as it was, and my mum had her hands full with the little ones. I doubt I'll be missed." Brigit found she didn't care for those particular words when she heard them coming out of her own mouth.

"Hmm," Bone murmured, considering. The braids of his beard tickled along the skin above her collar, and she felt him bend his head at his next words, a set of warm lips speaking against the side of her throat. "Perhaps ye were needed … elsewhere."

Now what does he mean by … ?

A kiss, and then a second, whispered at her neck. Something immaterial in her belly flipped and twisted. She set the knife back down. Brigit was no stranger to handling a blade, but just now it seemed to be an incredibly distracting time to be waving one around.

A huge, callused palm slid down her forearm and covered her right hand where it now lay atop the block. His thumb grazed across the side of her forefinger. Blood rushed in her ears. This game was at an end.

Before, it was a simple matter of him standing far too close. Now this man, this pirate with a great many more years' experience than Brigit, was pinning her against the tall cutting block with his body, the hand at her waist splayed and pulling her close rather than merely lingering at her hip.

"Mr Bone?" It was all she could do to rasp out the words.

He laced the fingers of his right hand together with hers in a move that spoke of both possession and reassurance. His mouth was moving down to her shoulder and she could feel him now, unavoidably hard against her backside.

Brigit was not accustomed to being touched this way by a man. Caressed. Savoured. Gooseflesh broke out over her arms, the tops of her breasts.

"Mr Bone." Her eyes were closed now under his touch. He brought her right hand up, the one he held in his, and placed it behind his shaven head. She allowed it to stay when he loosed his grip, and her fingertips trailed cool lines over the back of his neck.

Wasn't she supposed to be peeling potatoes? How had they managed to—

The feel of his fingertips on the far side of her jaw scattered her thoughts aside and a gentle nudge turned her face just a hair further in his direction. Unexpectedly soft lips and a brush of beard were at her ear, her cheek.

Heaven help you Brigit, what will you do if he …

He melted his lips against the very corner of her mouth. Not a full kiss, but a hint of one, and he lingered there, allowing her to take in the way her hand was still on the back of his neck and the way the cutting block forced her bottom back against his arousal. She felt his chest expanding at her back with his breath, which seemed to be coming just as erratic as her own, now.

"It's about time, Mrs O'Creagh," he said, with a renewed squeeze at her waist. She could barely summon words.

"Time?" The question sounded tiny and fearful. "Time for what?"

"Timc to feed a ship full of hungry men," he said, and her racing thoughts cleared as she heard the wry grin in his words.

He gave her a final squeeze and stepped back. Brigit wanted to collapse to the floor.

An entire *ship* full? It was taking all her efforts to contend with the *one* hungry man she'd already found. Brigit shifted her weight and felt a wet sliding between her legs. There would be nothing left of her by the next port, if this man devoured her the way his kisses at her throat said he intended.

She let out a long, shuddering sigh.

The rest of these potatoes would have to wait.

The curious texture of ship's biscuit ground between her teeth, softened as it was by a prolonged dip in the stew Bone had prepared. Brigit worked through the remains of her meal, leaning against the now ubiquitous cutting block once again. She thought if she sat, she might never want to rise again.

A crew of just over eighty sailors, most of them awake for the evening meal, had filed into the galley to receive their ration before moving off to the mess. *If it can properly be called such,* the cook had explained to her. Apparently the 'mess' consisted of a number of tables which folded down at the crew's convenience on the upper gun deck.

Bone had put her in charge of pouring the nightly ration of beer into the sailors' proffered mugs on their way out of the galley. Fist after fist came thrusting at her, each gripping a different sort of container. Metal, horn, fired clay, and most all well-worn. She'd lifted and refilled her pitcher from the barrel again and again, and imagined the line of men might never end.

Many of them had made crude comments, but in the trance of the moving queue, the repetitive actions, their words became a fog. Pour, pour, pour, refill, repeat.

When there were no more men, no more mugs offered, she'd stood there blinking as though she'd awakened from a dream.

It was her and the cook's turn to eat at last, and whilst she'd remained standing, he'd chosen to pull up a low stool and balance his plate on a knee. She wondered if it hurt for him to put weight for long periods of time on his wooden leg. And a considerable weight she suspected it must be. The man was built like an ox.

Now that it was quiet again in the galley, and she could indulge her curiosity while Bone's attention was on his meal, Brigit noted the dark wood that served the cook as a leg was worked in a detailed relief. She couldn't make out all the designs, but the larger ones appeared to pay tribute to a life at sea. A ship she could see from her vantage point, and an anchor. Possibly what may have been a mermaid.

"See something ye fancy?"

Her eyes jerked away from the carvings to meet the sky blue gaze of the cook. He'd caught her staring, but the quirking of one side of his mouth told her he wasn't upset by it. Still, she felt the need to apologise.

"I'm sorry Mr Bone, I shouldn't stare."

"Never ye mind, Mrs O'Creagh. I was only having a bit of fun." He leaned forward, an elbow on his knee, and cocked his head at her, mirth twinkling from frank, appreciative eyes.

The way he held her gaze without appearing to be distracted by the scarring dashed across her face made a fluttering giddiness beneath her stays she hadn't known since the earliest infatuations of her youth. Brigit still didn't understand why he persisted in addressing her in such a formal manner, though. She was, by all accounts, not much more than a scullery maid at this point.

In an unusually nervous effort to be polite, and perhaps out of a healthy fear of her own thoughts in the silence, she ventured a question.

"Did you … did you do the work yourself, Mr Bone? The carvings?" She didn't understand the tentative voice coming out of her, now. How had this man cowed her normal bold tongue?

"Oh, aye." His face broadened in a quiet smile of pride as he looked down at the wood himself, running blunt, reverent fingertips over his handiwork. "When a man spends a great deal of time at sea, he finds himself with just that: a great deal of time on his hands. Cooking doesn't take *all* day, ye know."

Bone brought his eyes up, grinning at her, before his attention darted off to her right.

"Get over here, you!"

Brigit stood straighter with a grunt of confusion and looked about herself. Was he talking to—?

From the corner of her eye, a stout ginger cat appeared, wending its way towards the cook. It made sure to rub its face over every standing thing in the galley along the way, including Brigit's shins through her skirt, before presenting itself to Bone with an arched back and slitted green eyes.

The cook delivered the expected scratching to the furry head and haunches, and Brigit suppressed a giggle at the sight of this enormous man catering to the whims of a single cat.

"And who's this, then?" she asked, setting her empty plate behind her atop the block.

"Ah, this'll be King George," he said, making the name sound unsuitably grand. "He keeps the rats at bay, though ye wouldn't know it as much time as he spends asleep under the steps in here." Bone dropped a morsel of salt pork on the deck and the mouser saw to it directly.

His words about the cat raised a worry she'd put aside much earlier in the day. A problem made far thornier after the way he'd cornered her before evening meal.

"Mr Bone ... where will *I* sleep?"

Blue eyes came up to meet hers again at this, interest in the cat forgotten at once. She felt the frank consideration in his gaze adding colour to her cheeks; men did not look at Brigit O'Creagh this way.

He rose from the stool, his ascent taking what seemed like days, reminding her again of his size. Weight on his good leg, his eyes travelled in a deliberate, earthy path from her face all the way down to her feet and back again. He took a slow, rolling step in her direction.

"That is a *very* good question, Mrs O'Creagh." He'd pulled back the pace of his speech to a languorous crawl. His next step followed with the soft rap of wood on wood. Brigit wrestled with the urge to shiver.

"I've been asking it myself since the captain saw us in the council chamber." His words came low and laden with insinuation as he closed the remaining distance between them with a lazy fluidity. She felt her hands draw back to rest on the edge of the block behind her, for what purpose she didn't know.

Are you going to vault backwards over the bloody thing, girl?

With a final step, he had her trapped again between his broad frame and the infernal cutting block. He looked down at her then with a maddeningly placid expression and a single arched brow.

"Where *will* ye sleep? Brigit?"

They were close enough now that his words vibrated from his chest into hers, and she was very aware of the rise and fall of her breasts as they pillowed above her neckline. From his vantage point, there was no way he hadn't noticed.

"I … I don't …" She stammered, unable to form a coherent answer, held in thrall as she was by this man.

"We'll worry about that matter in a moment," he said, voice pitched for her ears alone, "but first …"

Before the startled squawk of protest left her throat, Bone had gripped her about the waist with both hands and hoisted her bodily up and backwards. She now sat atop the cutting block.

Another step brought him right up against its edge, and when Brigit gaped down at her new position she saw that she hadn't the presence of mind to draw her legs properly to one side. The cook stood between her knees and there would be no bringing them closed now. Even an attempt would merely squeeze them against his hips.

This man wanted things from her. Things, Brigit admitted, she might even be willing to give, but her insides tightened with panic all the same. Pirates didn't earn their reputations through acts of charity and kindness. And a ship wasn't a very large place in which to run, if he was bent on doing her harm.

He leaned in, hands on either side of her knees, eyes hooded with … With what? Was that … *desire?* She wasn't sure. It wasn't the usual revulsion or loose tolerance she caught in the eyes of the few men who'd bedded her in the past. Cautious as a fawn at a forest's edge, she attempted to draw him out.

"But first?" Her eyes were wide, holding his, her body tense and still. What would he do? Would he hurt her?

"First," he said, in tones that spoke of endless time to spare, "I have another question I'd like answered." Their noses were whisper close now, but she didn't want to draw away. Her heart laboured with a wild hammering in her chest.

"What's that?" She was almost inaudible, her words falling like feathers on the ruddy beard brushing at her chin. She blinked at him. Their lips were so very close.

"Brigit . . ." He laid her name down as the lightest caress, and closed his eyes.

His mouth was on hers in a blanket of warmth. Not demanding, not lewd. A question. An offer.

She accepted.

A further tilt of her neck and she moulded her lips up against his. A low groan rumbled up from his chest and it carried the song of a man left hungry for far too long. The deep, male sound of want made her breath catch, and the parting of her lips seemed a signal to him.

His tongue slid over her lower lip, another request for permission, and she opened, admitting the caress. For the briefest moment, the novelty left her stunned. These were not the sort of kisses she'd received from other men. In fact, those had hardly been any sort of kisses at all. Her worries disintegrated under the mouth of this pirate standing between her knees, and she felt an appetite swell up in their place, tight and full to the point of bursting.

Brigit answered him back in kind, tasting, pushing up into his mouth with her own tongue. This brought another growl from the man and, as they pressed in to sample each other, she felt a heavy hand glide up the back of her neck and lace into her hair at the nape. Another languorous stroke of his tongue at that same moment brought her attention to the heat simmering between her thighs.

A heat lodged against the waist of a man who seemed intent on consuming her whole.

Her head was swimming by the time Bone drew back from the kiss, and when her eyes came open to meet his, she found them searching her with a desperate fever. She had no words and could merely stare at him and attempt to breathe.

Never before had a man caused Brigit to feel this way. The strands of white threaded through his beard, the extra lines at his brow absent from the faces of younger men she'd dallied with, did nothing to quell the spiralling tension at her centre. The more deliberate way he handled her, perhaps a result of his age, was possibly even heating her further.

He can take whatever he wants, at this point.

Whatever he sought in her eyes, he appeared to find, because he descended on her again, this time urgent, greedy. His mouth pulled at hers, tongue inviting her in, drawing small, frustrated sounds of need from the back of her throat to join his own. The hand at her neck trailed down along her back before the cook returned his palm to the block, bracing himself on both arms once again.

Her jaw received his kisses now, and then her ear, her neck. She tilted her head away, giving him better access, and her lips parted as he took it and moved lower, lapping at the hollow of her throat. Somewhere in the fog of sensation, she noticed her knees were not merely parted by this man who was fast devouring her sanity, but that without realising it, she'd shifted on the block to fit her hips directly against his obvious arousal. Layers of skirts and petticoats, a set of breeches and a shirt, were all that lay between them.

Brigit hated the captain a trifle less now, for having handed her off to this cook.

He was nipping at her collar bone, lips and teeth tracing a fiery path, and his right hand was back, urging the fabric of her sleeve further down over her shoulder. A rough thumb smoothed over the top of the crease where her arm met her body, and his kisses moved from there to her neckline. Between her thighs, a dull, warm throb made demands.

"Mr Bone ..." His name came without thought, a sigh

as her own right hand smoothed up over the arm that remained supporting the big man's weight.

"John ... if ye like ..." he said, amid intent nuzzling and lapping at her flesh.

So. John Bone it was. Pirate aboard *The Devil's Luck*.

He buried his face nose-deep between her breasts where they were piled high together by her stays and inhaled, letting out a groan of approval before his eager mouth set to work there as well.

Pirate. Cook. I don't care what he is, so long as he doesn't stop.

The man setting her body aflame soon became dissatisfied with the limitations set by her bodice and, with a grunt of frustration and a sharp tug, brought the entire affair some inches lower. Her remaining intact sleeve slid off its shoulder with the movement, and the bones of her stays prodded down into the meat of her hips. But now her breasts were completely freed and none of that mattered.

Bone righted himself and held her at arm's length for a moment, taking in her freckled curves with those blue eyes of his. The pale pink of her nipples darkened, hardening under the raw need in his stare alone.

"Mmm. Look at *that*," he said in the way a man might appraise a holiday feast. Brigit watched him chew at the inside of his lip and give a soft, disbelieving shake of his head before he bent to her once more, making new claims on her exposed flesh.

"John!" The newly-learnt name burst out of her with a gasp as he took one of her nipples into his mouth, plumping the breast around it with a warm squeeze of his hand.

Hot, wet suckling drew her in, and a hand moved over her other breast, palming its weight, brushing its stiffened tip with an idle thumb. Just as her head began to loll back in indulgence, however, she felt him pull away and stand again.

She opened her eyes to find him grinning down at her.

"Stay where ye are, Brigit O'Creagh," he said in a lusty taunt, flashing his teeth at her. "Don't. Move. Not one inch."

He left her dishevelled there, hair mussed, bare bosom pointing at the ceiling of the galley, while he stole through the pantry door on the aft wall. Crockery rasped over wood and paper crinkled from somewhere in the little room as the cook rummaged through Heaven knew what.

Brigit sat with her thighs splayed under her skirts, feeling wanton indeed without the distraction of wandering male hands or a mouth to make her forget her lewd position. Her nerves nearly had the better of her, and she was a heartbeat away from hopping down when Bone reappeared with a sly smile on his face.

A squat, stoppered clay jar fit just in his palm and he held it up to her as he made his way back to the block. He came between her knees again and set the jar down on the cutting surface beside her hip, prying out its wide cork as he went.

She peered down into the container and saw it full of something glossy and amber-coloured.

"What's this?" she asked him, curiosity and apprehension bubbling away inside her.

Bone pressed his forefinger into the jar and came out with a smudge of the stuff coating the tip. He lifted his hand between them, the raised finger poised to touch her lips.

"Open."

Brigit screwed up her face. He expected her to put whatever this was in her mouth on faith?

"Go on." He gave her an amused half-smile. "It won't be bad, I promise ye."

Narrowing her eyes at him, she decided to trust. He'd shown her only pleasure so far. She let her jaw relax and her lips parted. Bone slid the finger inside. As it came in contact with her tongue, sweetness flooded her mouth.

Honey.

His grin grew wider as he saw the recognition on her face. Brigit closed her lips around the treat he offered and used her tongue to clean the rest of the sticky goodness away, slowing down her movements while she held his gaze. She knew just what it would look like, and this small display rekindled some of her normal boldness.

A controlled hiss from the cook told her his imagination had conjured the only possible image it could, and he pulled back the finger with a wet pop.

"My private store," he explained with a grin, "so don't ye be telling anyone about it, Mrs O'Creagh."

She chuckled at this. "You mean I shouldn't gather the crew 'round and tell them tales of how I came to know about their cook's private things?"

"Such cheek." He tried to be serious while blue eyes twinkled. His forefinger caught her under the chin and tilted her jaw that he might claim another kiss. "Ought to have ye ... over my knee," he said between distracted bites at her lower lip. "The good one, no less."

Despite the rumbling jest in his tone, something exciting and dangerous crackled over her skin at the pictures this painted in her head. But there was no time for stray thoughts.

The hand went again to the jar, and this time his thumb came out bearing the honey. In a deliberate move, he cradled her breast and transferred the sweet glaze in a smudge over her nipple. Mischief alight in his eyes as he watched her reaction to this move, he did the same in turn to the other.

Are all ships' cooks such decadent madmen?

"Now," he said, eyes on his handiwork, "what finer thing could a man ask for?" With a satisfied nod to himself, Bone fell to her upturned breasts once more.

His first exploratory taste of them, she discovered, had been a mere shadow of the attention he gave to her now. The tight, honeyed bud found itself pulled into his mouth, the sensation gentle at first while his tongue rasped away the sweetness he'd laid there, but then more insistent as he worked to clean away every trace.

She could scarcely believe the sight of him at her breast. He looked a different man entirely than the imposing pirate she'd first seen in the council chamber. Not fearsome at all now that his eyes were closed in pleasure and quiet rumbles of appreciation drifted up over her moistened flesh.

Brigit bit her lip as her eyes moved down to his shoulders, their depth from front to back making her want to knead and push at them. The awkward young men who made up her limited past experiences had been all elbows and shoulder blades. John Bone was a great, solid beast of a man. A man whose weight she wanted to be smothered in, who made her want to roll about like a cat in heat. She would've been massaging and pawing away at him, if only she had sufficient hold of her faculties at that moment to do anything other than support her weight on her arms and be savoured.

When she thought there could truly be no more, he moved to the other side and began the process anew, relieving a second sensitive tip of its sugary coating. The suckling at this side grew almost painful as his mouth demanded more. The first nipple he'd worked at had been damp and cooling in the air of the galley, but now he took it up between his fingers, rolling and tugging. The parallel sensations worked to drag urgent whimpers from her throat.

"Please, John …" The words tumbled out of her, though she didn't know precisely what it was she wanted from him. Only to beg perhaps. Beg for more.

Hearing his own name seemed to further stoke the fires of his kisses, and he carried them scorching up along her throat again until his lips found their way to hers. His mouth demanded for a final, clear moment, that Brigit O'Creagh acknowledge what was happening down here in the galley of *The Devil's Luck*.

And what was happening was that she wanted this man,

this pirate, to sweep her up and carry her along to all the forbidden places she'd never been.

He appeared to be well on his way to doing just that.

Righting himself, he rested his forehead atop hers and moved broad palms into a light grip just above either of her knees. She angled her head back to look up at him, thoughts spinning even as her breath slowed.

Before today, Brigit couldn't have imagined blue eyes would remind her of fire.

With a squeeze of his thumbs, and a sliding shift of his hands a mere inch higher on her thighs, John Bone made his most dangerous promise yet. She exhaled in a silent groan that threatened to turn her wrong side out. The bare hint of a smirk on his face spoke of wickedness to come.

"Care to show me what you're hiding 'neath these skirts, pretty girl?"

The coarse edge on his voice teased and suggested, made the floor seem to drop away, leaving her falling, untethered.

What else could he teach her, down here in the dim light of this galley?

She slid her own fingers under his and, without releasing his stare—she didn't know how she'd maintain her courage if she looked away—began to gather up the several layers of fabric between her and the intentions of this man she'd known for mere hours.

Inch by inch her hemline rose, until she felt the brush of air against her thighs above the top edge of her stockings. A handful or two of material further and the bulk of her garment was gathered at her waist. Bone stepped back and she swallowed, fearing his reaction now that they'd come this far.

The first thing he did then was the last thing she expected.

He didn't reach for her secrets now that she'd laid herself bare. He didn't pull back to leer at her, either.

Brigit felt each of her wrists covered by a hand and, with his eyes still on hers, Bone drew his touch in a tortuous place up along her arms. Over her shoulders he went, fingertips a whisper, until he cupped her jaw from both sides, thumbs brushing her cheekbones. Tracing over her scars. She wanted to avert her eyes, but found she could not.

Again, he kissed her. Only this time, despite the slow care in his touch, Brigit felt the way the tips of his fingers curled under just so, the way the muscles in his arms were tight beneath her hands where they'd risen to rest during the kiss. Here was a man barely restrained, schooling himself to patience with all of his will. His tension was bleeding over into her body, curling her toes within her slippers.

Were that not enough, as he'd moved close again during the kiss, her newly bared and humming flesh had been pressed right up against the blatant desire tightening his breeches. He was not small.

Brigit whimpered, overwhelmed with the still intensity of the moment, and the noise from her made Bone inhale sharply through his nose as they kissed. He was moments away from losing his grip on control, she could feel it.

One of his hands slid away from her face and moved lower. Her heart sped and fluttered. Warm male fingers came between them, setting her nerves on fire. She was soaked, and now he knew it.

Bone pulled back from the kiss, eyes fierce with arousal, and stole his first glance down to where his fingertips slid. He drew his hand back enough to glide thumb and forefinger together, sampling her wetness and giving a tiny shake of his head. A slow grin spread over his face and he met her eyes again.

"It's almost as if you've taken a fancy to me, Mrs O'Creagh."

Had she not been strung taut as a bow at that moment, Brigit would have laughed. The best she could do was turn some furious shade of red.

She almost fell forward when he took an abrupt, long step back from her. In a skilful move, he hooked his foot behind a leg of the low stool he'd sat on before, drew it near, and sat, scooting closer as he did.

His face was just of a height with the edge of the tall cutting block. The one on which she was perched. Splayed. Showing him all of her secrets. She held her breath.

In a sudden move, John Bone took both her thighs in his grip, right where they met her hips, and his face dove straight for her centre. He stopped, however, just short of making contact. She exhaled in a rush of air. Lord, but this man was skilled at toying with her.

One of his hands moved in, and she started a bit when his thumb made the first inevitable contact. He passed over her lips with it, dipping into the moisture he found there.

"I don't think we'll need any honey down here, lass," he murmured.

Turning his head, he set his mouth high along the inside of her thigh and began to kiss and nip at her. The thumb took up a lazy circling between her legs and she found herself mumbling quiet affirmations by the time he'd moved his lips to the other leg.

"Mmm … yes, John … please …"

When he first nuzzled his nose against the modest patch of curls above her sex, she almost didn't notice, floating in a sensory fog as she was. His tongue on her, however, almost had her jumping straight up into the air. Heavy palms at her thighs kept her in place, though, and the pirate who'd seduced her out of her skirts in less than a day began to eat.

Brigit knew of this act, but only from gossip she'd heard from other young women. Mostly the pretty ones who had the faces that could charm a lover into doing anything they wanted. None of the men *she'd* entertained had ever asked to do any such thing. More often they seemed to prefer she bend over, face away, and spread her legs in the dark. Hers was not a face men dreamt of.

Now there was light, dim though it was, from an oil lamp in the galley, and what she saw was at the edge of her comprehension.

Bone had his mouth buried in the folds of her sex. His tongue danced and delved and rasped. Every nook, every hidden crevice of her pink, swollen flesh … all new subjects of his thorough exploration. She felt her hips beginning to roll, an instinctive response to pleasure's pull.

With a shift on the stool, he brought a hand under her right knee and hoisted her thigh over his shoulder so she could relax and rest it there. Her left leg he allowed to dangle where it was, but she was held quite wide apart for him this way.

There was nowhere for her to hide, parted as she was, no place for shame. Nothing to do but allow this man to take her every measure, the pull of his lips and even teeth drawing from her sensations she'd had no idea were possible.

She allowed herself to bring her hand up to his shoulder, running her fingertips along the side of his neck, the top of an ear while he worked at unravelling her sanity. It was a feeling unlike anything she'd known, his tongue playing over her lips, sliding along that furrow between her thighs, catching at the swollen bead that made her whimper with every pass. It was altogether wetter, more unpredictable than her own fingers, which she'd so sinfully used on herself in the past, and she found herself pressing into his attentions now, wanting whatever more there was he had to give.

A different sort of touch joined the lusty strokes of his tongue, then. Something firmer smoothing over the silk of her entrance.

Speaking of fingers …

Her breath caught in her throat for a moment before shuddering out in a rush. Bone toyed with her, circling the pad of a finger through her moisture, occasional teasing sallies suggesting he might even intend to—

"Uunngh!"

The noise he startled out of her was almost a question, and the gasp that immediately followed was a sound she'd never heard herself make. The cook had filled her in one smooth motion with a thick forefinger, and was now sliding it lazily along the inner walls of her channel.

He glanced up at her then, a satisfied smirk on his face as she continued to sputter and whine over this new sensation.

"Ye like that then, do ye?"

"Mmmhmm." She chewed at her lower lip, nodding urgently.

How much more confirmation could a man need? Haven't I wet his knuckles enough?

"Right." He chuckled at her frustration. "Let's see to ye, shall we?"

See to me? What does he—

"Auugh!"

His mouth fell on her again, lips latching over her swollen flesh, and her world lit on fire. The finger inside took up its swirl and plunge again, and John Bone began to orchestrate the most heavenly assault on her senses.

Self-control bid her farewell. Brigit felt as though she'd been tied to a horse whose backside had been slapped and she was now careening forward through unstoppable pleasure, unable to clutch even the tiniest branch along the way to help her slow down.

There was an awkward wriggle between her legs for the briefest of moments which made the beginnings of a question go flying by in her mind. A renewed pushing made her grasping sheath tight. Bone had added a second finger, and she was now doubly full.

She gritted out a strangled moan at this, but he was not finished. The tips of his fingers curled up, and as he dragged them out again …

"John!"

Brigit nearly exploded on his hand.

What is he doing *to me?*

The strokes continued, and his fingertips raked over some seed of pleasure she didn't know she had, the pull of his mouth again added in, making her cry out with startled enjoyment.

"That's it, girl." His words of encouragement came low between bouts of determined suckling. "Show me. Show me what ye want."

She began to truly whine and writhe, her bottom flexing atop the block and her sex grinding up into Bone's mouth and hand. Her noises grew more desperate as she abandoned caution. He laughed and nipped at her a bit to draw her attention.

"Bite yer lip, Mrs O'Creagh, or you'll have half the crew down here."

The reality he painted set her into the briefest moment of panic and she choked back her moans into a tighter staccato of urgent whimpers and grunts. Though how long she could go on like this in relative silence, her pussy burning with need and pins and needles coming into her toes, she didn't know. Surely not much longer.

"Now, Brigit," he said. "Show me."

His busy hand turned so that his palm faced her thigh instead of the ceiling and, before there was time to question, a new fingertip was circling at another entrance.

Lips and tongue lapping and pulling, fingers plumbing within, and now this unfamiliar massaging press at her tight, hidden pucker. It became too much all at once and Brigit burst apart into a million tiny pieces.

Her mouth fell open in a silent scream, some remote part of her remembering Bone's caution for quiet, but she made up for it by clutching at the fabric of his shirt at his shoulder, her right heel digging into his upper back. Her hips rolled of their own accord as she grated her fluttering, soaking sex over his mouth, riding out her climax, wringing it of every last drop.

It was the most beautiful thing she'd ever felt, and it happened here. In the galley of a pirate ship, at the touch of a man probably wanted for crimes in every respectable port.

He looked up at her then, as she floated down from her peak and the muscles in her thighs began to relax.

A man whose blue eyes and merry smile were starting to make her knees weak, it seemed.

Bone placed a final, reverent kiss atop her little patch of curls before taking hold of her hem and lowering her skirts back into place. She gaped at him.

"My God, John! What *was* that?"

He stood with a grin, pushing the stool away again with his good leg.

"What?" he asked in a teasing rumble. "Ye think a man my size doesn't know how to eat?"

The disbelieving laugh that burst out of her then at such a comment was interrupted at once by Bone's mouth catching hers up again in a victorious kiss. She realised with a start she could taste herself on him, but entirely failed to care. His arms circled her shoulders, crushing her into him, and she gave back his kiss with a passion of her own.

Brigit O'Creagh knew in that moment she would peel potatoes to outnumber the stars if it allowed her this each time, after. Board a thousand pirate ships if there would only be a galley on each of them where John Bone wanted to kiss her. To Hell with Boston, or Bristol, or even Cork. This could be home. Maybe.

Still, a question remained unanswered. She looked up at the man who stood between her thighs and reminded him of where they'd left off before they'd been … distracted.

"Mr Bone," she said, "you've yet to tell me where I'm to sleep."

Chapter 2

Peg Legs and Pretty Girls

"No matter how plain a woman may be, if truth and honesty are written across her face, she will be beautiful."

— Eleanor Roosevelt

The hold was seldom a quiet place, not at this late hour and full of snoring sailors, but the maid lying next to him seemed to have little problem falling and staying asleep, despite the noise. John lay on his back, fingers laced together over his belly, awake and trying to ignore the tempting, warm body to his left.

It was dark in the space where most of the crew hung their hammocks, save for a lone oil lamp which was kept alight so men could rise in the dark, if need be, and not stumble about and disturb their mates. The air was close, as could be expected from a space full of unwashed men, and he was unsatisfied with the notion of bringing the young woman along to bed down there, but there were no other acceptable alternatives.

The only other woman aboard was surely sleeping in the captain's stateroom, so there would be no sending Brigit O'Creagh to sleep with her. If he left her to make up a bed in the galley she'd be left alone, and that would never do. He knew there were members of the crew who would sneak into the kitchens with an idea that they were being so very clever, to pilfer a midnight ration, and he wouldn't leave her in there to be alone for one of them to come blundering in and find something other than the normal fare available for their perusal.

His sudden protectiveness for the girl made him screw up his face in the dark.

What is she to ye, John Bone? Ye met her only this morning, and now ye worry about protecting her honour? Who protected her from you?

The thought made him cringe, but only for a moment. She'd hardly seemed unwilling. In fact, her kisses told quite the opposite story. And the way she'd said his name … Again his breeches were becoming unnecessarily tight. She shifted in her sleep, her back to him, and he fought off the urge to roll onto his side and cover her in greedy hands and pent up lust. That seemed the way to treat a whore and he was beginning to realise he didn't think of the young Brigit that way.

John let his head turn towards her dim outline. Her sleeping form faced the interior wall of the hull and some instinct had made him place himself between her and the rest of the sleeping crew. She hadn't argued for a moment when he'd led her down here, nor when he showed her the narrow platform they would need to share. She'd simply nodded, settled in, and was gone to the world within moments.

His was the only low berth of its kind in the cramped hold. In a skirmish aboard a ship Captain Blackburn had led them against some seven years gone, another man had fallen atop him while he descended a stair into their lower gun deck. The weight of the other man had driven his leg between the steps where it twisted, breaking the bone clean in two. An infection and amputation later, and he found himself promoted to Cook. Not only were his days of boarding and fighting over, but so were the nights he could navigate the trickery of a hammock. Mr Adams, the cooper and John's friend after so many years at sea, had suggested a platform be erected and a thin, straw-stuffed mattress procured for the ship's new cook, and the quartermaster had approved the plan.

And now, tonight, it was *because* of his lost limb and not in spite of it, he had a place for an appealing young maid to bed down beside him. John wondered as he made valiant efforts to keep his hands to himself, if it were not luckier that he *had* broken the leg. If he were a whole man, someone else would be cook. Someone else would have heard her bold, easy laughter. Buried his face in that freckled bosom of hers, or lifted her skirts and brought out those lovely sounds.

Or perhaps someone else would *not* have treated her so well. John knew then that he wanted to protect her from any other man who might even think of treating her poorly.

After one day? Ye have it bad, John.

Yes, perhaps he was getting a bit caught up in the idea of a woman allowing his advances without having seen the inside of a purse first. Most men of the sort that crewed *The Devil's Luck* were accustomed to paying for a night's affection, and that went doubly so for a man missing part of a leg. It had been years since he'd wooed anyone by his own charm, if that was truly what had happened today in the galley. And yet Brigit didn't seem like the sort of girl who would part her legs for just any man.

No matter what sort of woman she was, Brigit O'Creagh was doing a fine job of keeping him awake. He needed to sleep. There would be plenty of time tomorrow for chewing on thoughts such as these.

John settled into his usual routine of fighting off wakefulness and began imagining what places his life would have taken him if he'd never taken to piracy in the first place. Soon, however, those fantasies gave way to musings of what more he would do with the lovely little maid, if she showed an interest. Sleep took him all the same, though for once John Bone had a smile on his face when it did.

As always, he awoke before the sun. The hold was quieter now that most of the first watch had made their way above decks, and John's meagre bed was warmer than normal. As his waking mind assembled his surroundings, he realised that this was because there was a soft young body nestled up against his. The next thing he realised was that, as it did every morn', his prick had risen with the dawn, as well. Only on this day found it pressed between himself and a lovely round bottom instead of pointed at the ceiling.

It seemed at some point during the night he'd rolled onto his side and Brigit had fitted her back against his chest. His right arm had conspired to drape itself over her waist, pulling her close. His left arm was … gone? No. He smirked to himself. It was under her head and completely numb.

For a long moment he lay there, indulging in the simple pleasure of inhaling her scent and trying not to grind himself against her. At least not any more than she'd notice.

What a fine way to begin a man's morning!

He didn't want to wake her, but if his sense of time served him correctly, as it usually did, he'd an idea of how today might begin on a different note in light of his guest.

"Mrs O'Creagh," he murmured against her ear, trying not to startle her, but to stir her awake all the same. She let out a faint, sleepy grunt of contentment and huddled further into the curve of his body, lacing her fingers through his and drawing his arm tighter about her. He bit back a groan as her backside wriggled against him. This would never do. At least not yet.

"Brigit," he said, with more volume and clarity. That did it.

She awoke with a sharp intake of air. He felt her whole body stiffen, out of fear or confusion, he wasn't sure which.

Please don't make a scene down here, girl.

John had no interest in hearing the inevitable taunts from the remaining men in the hold, the snide offers of help to subdue an unruly woman, should she raise a fuss.

The maid released a sigh that seemed to indicate she remembered where she was and melted back into his embrace.

"Mmm ... John," she mumbled, to his relief and pleasant surprise.

"Good morning, pretty girl," he said, venturing a light kiss at the top of her ear. She didn't object, though she made no move to rouse herself.

"It's early," the groggy maid said into flesh of his numb arm.

"Yes it is, girl." John drew the cold limb out from under her neck and began the awkward process of rubbing out the pins and needles. "But let's awake all the same. I'd like to show ye something."

She was stirring at his words now, stretching her small body in a most pleasing arch before sitting up on the narrow platform, her hands moving to smooth over sleep-mussed hair.

The maid watched him with curiosity as he went about fitting the end of his leg into the wood and leather socket, buckling the mess of straps in a greater hurry than usual with her eyes on him. John Bone wanted pity from no one, least of all this woman who'd woken up in his bed.

False leg in place, he heaved himself upright, wincing as he put weight on it. He'd taught himself to move about without a crutch, but it was still at the high end of uncomfortable, especially in the mornings. But now was no time to complain. Brigit was looking at him with expectant eyes.

"Come on, then," he said in a low voice, mindful of the few men who still slept. She followed him out of bed at his gesture and he turned and moved towards the stair.

For once, a day was brimming with possibility and they hadn't fired a single cannon.

A good start, this.

John hummed to himself as the young maid trailed along after him.

The haze of sleep wore off quickly as the cook led her about the ship. Brigit caught the curious stares of the crew, already working at their watch in the blue pre-dawn light, and felt her cheeks colour in response. Surely some of them had seen Bone bring her to sleep in his bed last night, and barring that, had seen her lying fitted against him, merry as you please, this morning.

Those thoughts aside, it *had* been a pleasant way to wake up, she admitted to herself. Warmth at her back, a heavy male arm draped over her. If only he'd stop calling her 'pretty girl', she'd have no complaint at all. It made her feel odd. She'd seen a mirror; knew what she was. Perhaps without the scars … but his silly names for her were more likely born out of the shameless way she'd behaved yesterday than anything else.

Maybe shameless, but you liked it well enough, didn't you?

After a much needed trip to the head, she fell in behind him again and followed. Brigit listened to the sound of his steps on the deck, one quiet and one a wooden thud, and wondered what it was he wanted her to see. They arrived at the port side gunwale amidships and he came to a halt, placing his hands on the heavy railing. Unsure of what to do, she mimicked his posture and followed his gaze out into the slowly brightening distance.

"What are we looking at, Mr Bone?" Her words were quiet in the cool morning air. Though most of the crew was already buzzing about, it seemed right to keep her voice down, as though the ship herself were some great beast she didn't want to awaken.

The cook stepped over and behind her, replacing his hands on the gunwale on either side of hers. Again, his immense warm body was at her back, just as it had been yesterday while she'd been peeling those infernal potatoes. Her pulse fluttered and flung the last of her sleepiness aside like a curtain.

Heaven help me, it may be too early for this.

"Have ye ever seen the sun rise while at sea, Mrs O'Creagh?"

She fairly melted back against him. He'd brought her up here to see a sunrise? What sort of pirate was he?

"No I haven't, Mr Bone," she said, still quiet.

"Then watch with me, lass," he said near her ear.

And watch they did. The sea was glassy and calm that morning, and the endless plane of water and dome of sparsely clouded sky had been quite blue and grey when they'd arrived. Now, as they stood there, saying nothing, the horizon grew brighter by the moment. The undersides of clouds began to blush as the first rays of the sun kissed them, its blazing head just out of sight.

Bone's forearms brushed against hers and she felt him lower his face. He didn't kiss her, though, or whisper anything. The lower edge of his jaw came into contact with her cheekbone and rested there: comfortable, but not demanding.

Comfortable. Yes, that was just how she felt. The first bright sliver of sun was edging past the line of blue now, and the sky was moving into shades of amber and gold. Standing here, taking in this sight with nothing in the way to block her view, the subtle rise and fall of the ship underfoot, Brigit realised that for once she had no questions. She didn't need to know anything. Once they left the railing, she'd be perfectly content to follow this man again to the galley, to prepare the meals, to listen to his stories and tell her own, perhaps be robbed of a kiss or two. The last two fingers of her right hand slid over the top of the cook's, and she felt his thumb nudge at them from below.

They'd been standing in companionable silence for some time, and the sun hung full and low now just above the horizon, a heavy, ripe fruit blazing against the few tufts of clouds in its path. It had reached the point where they had to start looking away.

"Very lovely, Mr Bone." It was all she could think of to say. She'd never been one for fancy words, and none she knew were the poetic sort suited to oceans and sunrises.

"So it is, Brigit," he said, drawing a hand across the small of her back as he stepped again to her side. "The Lord is good indeed that even a pirate may be permitted to look upon his lovely creation each morning." He caught her eye with these quiet words, and she found she could no more look directly at him when he said such things than she could at the sun.

"Shall we return to the galley then?"

She nodded, ready to busy herself with a task rather than continue to stand here and be stared at by the all-too-serious eyes of this red-bearded man.

"Then let us go to it, Mrs O'Creagh; we've a full day of work ahead."

His words were matter-of-fact, but his tone was gentle as he turned from the railing and set off across the deck. Brigit followed him again past crates and rigging and working sailors, to the now familiar hatch that opened down into the galley.

What did it mean, she wondered, that she went along again without objection, as though trailing the cook down into the belly of the ship were an old habit, and not a path she'd trod for the first time only yesterday? Or that she'd slept through a night without waking for the first time in who knew how long?

Who cares what everything means, girl? Stop daydreaming and keep your wits about you! This is a bloody pirate ship.

A massive pot of what was soon to be porridge was occupying most of the cook's attention as they made ready for the day's noon meal. Brigit busied herself with scrubbing the remaining plates she hadn't the time to finish washing the previous evening.

Too busy being someone else's dinner, were you?

She shook her head and glanced over at Bone. King George was rubbing his furry face over the man's wooden leg while the cook bent at the waist and tended to the fire inside the iron stove.

"So what were ye planning to do when ye got to Boston, Mrs O'Creagh? Stay on with the widow?" He straightened himself with a grunt and struck up their conversation again.

"I'm not sure," she admitted, bringing her eyes back to her work. "I don't know what Mrs Collingwood's living arrangements with her uncle were to be like; whether he had servants of his own she'd prefer. It seemed a thing to be decided after we arrived."

"And what if she no longer required yer services? What then?" He shooed the cat away with an absent flap of the rag he untucked from his belt.

Not that it mattered now, she thought. The captain had already relieved her of her duties to the widow. But a desire that Bone should continue speaking had her answering all the same.

"I would have offered to work for my passage back to Bristol aboard *The Mourning Dove*, I suppose. Or, if the captain had no use for me, perhaps find an inn at the port to serve in until I'd earned enough coin to pay my way back."

The cat had decided to look for attention at *her* feet now, and she reached down for a moment to scratch at a ginger ear with her wet hand. The little beast didn't seem to appreciate this and shook his head before stalking off to his place beneath the stair.

Bone was wiping his hands on the rag. "Ye don't seem to be much bothered to find yerself here instead of bound for Boston," he said, not making much of a question of it, though it seemed he hoped for a response.

"I'm quite used to matters not going the way I expect, Mr Bone," she said, scraping a dried bit of potato off a plate with her nail. "I've learned to make the best of what comes, and not to expect anything. That's how a body stays free from worry, as far as I can see."

He nodded at this, considering.

"Would ye like to see Nassau, Brigit?"

She looked up at him, blinking at his abrupt change of subject. Laying the last dish aside, she dried her own wet hands on her apron, following the big man across the room with her eyes as he moved to paw about in a drawer of utensils with a metallic clattering.

"Isn't that on an island somewhere?" she asked. "Is that where we're headed?"

"Jamaica, yes," he said, his voice ringing a bit louder in success as he brought out the ladle he'd been looking for, "and it *is* our next port."

"How long will it take us to get there?" she asked, moving to take up a broom that stood in the corner where the stair met the wall of the hull.

"Oh, several weeks at least, if the winds favour us and the sea is fair."

Several weeks?

It was not any longer than it might have taken them to sail to Boston, she supposed. One night aboard *The Devil's Luck*, however, had already taken her on a far different adventure than the boredom she'd expected from being cooped up with the widow.

Where would she find herself some weeks from now? Would John Bone be the only pirate she had to contend with? And who was to say she could handle *him?* People didn't always show their true colours straight away. There could be trouble yet from the man. Though so far her most pressing problem was her thoughts wandering back to the feel of his hands on her.

That's it, girl. Show me. Show me what ye want.

Brigit coloured as she remembered his words, and what was worse, he was making his way over to where she swept near the stair. She kept her eyes to the floor, but saw his hand grip the broom handle under hers, stilling her movement as he came to her side.

She didn't know what to expect when she raised her eyes to his, but she was glad to have a grip on the wooden handle, as her hands would have been shaking had they been empty.

The boyish grin she found spreading across his face, however, caught her off guard and she couldn't help the corners of her own mouth turning up at the sight.

"Would ye like me to show ye the port when we arrive, Brigit?"

Show her the port? What was he on about?

"We'll be leaving the ship?"

"Of course!" He laughed, sliding his fingers up the handle to cover hers. "We're not slaves, lass, we get shore leave. It's in the contract." He waggled his eyebrows at her, tilting his head down a bit as if he shared a great secret. She smiled further at his playful tone, and decided she could join in his mood.

"And what's so special about Nassau?" she teased, angling the broom out to the side, stretching both their arms along with it, forcing the two of them to step closer together. "I've seen ports before."

"Have ye?" he asked, voice moving low to meet her taunts. He tossed the broom to the side out of both their hands and caught her up at the waist as it clattered to the floor. She bent backwards slightly in his arms and became once again very aware of their bodies pressed together as he flashed her his teeth in a devious smile. "Nassau port is a pirate haven, Mrs O'Creagh. You'll want to stay *very* close by my side, if I'm to show ye around, lest some scallywag lay hands on ye."

His face was mere inches from hers now, and she clutched at the fabric of his shirt, lest she fall backwards, off balance as she was. Brigit's gaze flitted from his teasing eyes to his mouth and she swallowed to wet her own throat.

"No, we wouldn't want that now, would we?" Her voice came as a breath just before they came together at once, each relieved to find themselves again part of a kiss.

It was the same as yesterday: searing, heart-stopping, lovely. She could feel in the pull of his palms at her waist and the low needful sounds he made that said he, like Brigit, had been dancing around the idea of this very moment all morning, each unsure of how to approach the other again.

None of that mattered now, though, and they indulged in long moments of simple, delicious sensation.

When they parted at last, the kiss had left her without a thread of tension and neither could surrender their smiles. Bone nudged upward at her chin with a knuckle as he took half a step back to let her breathe.

"Besides," he said, eyes merry, "the islands are nothing like home. They're a paradise. White sand, sea the colour of a jewel, warm, sweet air."

His words reminded her of another curious thought.

"Where's home, Mr Bone?"

"Aside from decks of *The Devil's Luck*? Tynemouth, I suppose. But I haven't been back there in years." The cook rubbed a broad hand over the back of his neck at this and she suspected he didn't want to speak any more on the subject just now.

Tynemouth. It explained the accent, which she was growing to enjoy.

"I seem to have interrupted yer sweeping, Mrs O'Creagh," he pointed out, the trace of mischief still light on his tone. "I'll let ye return to it. I'm off to see Mr

Adams—our cooper," he said when he saw the blank look on her face, "about our fresh water supply. I'll be back before long and we should be nearly ready for noon meal."

"Upon your return then, Mr Bone," she said, retrieving the broom from where it had fallen. She wanted to go with him, but it would seem silly to trail him through the ship wherever he went like a lost lamb, so she took up her sweeping again.

"Brigit," he acknowledged her with a warm nod as he mounted the stair and disappeared up through the hatch.

She'd been busying herself about the wide planks of the galley floor some several minutes, gathering a neat pile of crumbs and dust together in one central spot, when she heard footsteps on the stair. Brigit looked up from the rhythm of her passes with the broom to see a man descending into the galley.

Mopping at her brow with the back of her hand, she stood straight and paused in her work, waiting for the sailor to see her there.

Now what does this one want?

By the time he reached the bottom step, his eyes had adjusted to the dimmer light of the galley and when they swung around and landed on Brigit he grinned.

"Ah, so *here's* the new cook's mate. You that lady's maid?" His lopsided smile split his face wider and he pushed the sleeves of his shirt back one at a time to reveal his forearms as he stepped further into the space.

"No longer, it seems," she answered, taking up her sweeping again with a wary eye for the inquisitive pirate.

Brigit imagined he might be a handful of years older than she was, and solidly built, if not nearly so vast as Mr Bone. His skin was surprisingly pale for a man of the sea, and watery blue eyes appraised her above a crude smirk. Lank, unwashed dark hair fell about his face at his cheekbones and jaw, and he shoved it back out of his eyes with a cocky hand.

"Name's William Platt," he said, making a gesture with his fingers near his forehead as though doffing an invisible hat. His eyes were on her as she moved and she tried to hide her complete lack of approval.

So, he's come to stare at the cook's new pet, has he?

"Brigit O'Creagh," she responded in kind. Short and polite seemed the best approach, forced though it was. No need to irritate a man when she didn't know if he had a temper.

"Where's our Mr Bone then?" he asked, glancing about.

"Off to see the cooper."

She allowed her work to take her around to the opposite side of the cutting block, caution nudging her to position the large piece of furniture between herself and this Platt.

He stood there eyeing her, weight on one leg and the other bent, thumbs hooked into the top edge of his breeches, all but pointing at his groin with his other fingers.

"Cap'n has that widow of yours locked away in his cabin, you know. Don't think he wants to share with the rest of us, Miss Brigit."

Miss Brigit? Miss? *What did he take her for? The ship's new whore?*

The first kindling of anger flared across her cheeks at his rude address, a fact Platt appeared to enjoy.

"No, I don't imagine he would." Her retort had the beginnings of cheek to it. She was more than ready now for this smug pirate to be away from the galley.

He sauntered over to the block and rested his weight on the heels of his palms on either corner, lewd gaze raking over her bosom as he stood there.

"Mr Bone's a generous man," he continued his taunt, leaning forward, "perhaps *he'll* see the rest of the crew gets a fair portion."

Brigit was standing still at this point, both hands with a tight grip on the broom handle, knuckles flexed. She'd spent her youth in a household with four brothers. While she wasn't keen on starting a fight, she bloody well knew how to finish one.

Just you make one move, William Platt.

The man wasn't entirely unpleasant to look at, she could admit, but in the span of a few minutes she'd already had enough of this arrogant prat. He'd have a scrap on his hands if he thought he was going to be getting any sort of "portion" of *her*.

"Mrs O'Creagh." A third voice joined them, along with the thump-step she'd come to know over the last day. "I've just heard that—Platt? What do ye want down here?"

Bone turned at the bottom of the stair and stepped into the galley. Her grip on the broom relaxed.

"Just thought I'd see if anything new had been added to the menu," the younger sailor said, eyes still plainly assessing the new potential for sport on the opposite side of the cutting block.

"Whatever gave ye that idea, Mr Platt?" The cook moved to stand just behind Brigit, one of his heavy hands rising to cover her shoulder in a possessive manner.

Some series of looks flew between the two men, Bone's end of which she couldn't see, and Platt ended it in a shrug and stepped back from the block, the mischievous grin still plastered across his pale face.

"Only thought I'd check, Bone," he said with a smirk, stepping back towards the stair. "A man never knows."

"Well now he does," the big man behind her said as the younger sailor mounted the steps. He gave her shoulder another squeeze.

"And Platt," he called after the other man who turned back for a moment at his words, "make sure the rest of the crew knows, as well. I don't expect to see anyone else down here making inquiries about the 'menu'. Ye follow?"

"All right, Bone, all right," he said, putting up his hands in mock surrender before he made his way up through the hatch.

She angled her face to look up at the cook then, and he narrowed his eyes in the direction of the stair, shaking his head. "Bloody Platt."

His curse made her giggle and she turned to face him as he lowered his eyes to hers.

"Look what happens," he said, tracing a knuckle along the side of her throat. "I leave a sweet unattended for but a few minutes and here they come, ready to get their hands into the honey jar. Are ye alright, Brigit?"

"I'm fine Mr Bone," she said, arching her neck against his touch, "though Mr William Platt may have grown a lump on his head if you'd been much longer." She gestured with the broom, and the deep sound of his laughter vibrated pleasantly through her chest.

"Perhaps I should have waited then! Now let's call these animals down for noon meal, pretty girl, I think this porridge is about ready."

Platt.

John shook his head to himself as he ladled out porridge to the line of sailors, keeping an eye on their hands to see that they didn't take more than the single piece of tack each as they passed.

Not a quarter of an hour he'd been gone and already one of them had come sniffing around like a dog looking for scraps. He had no specific dislike for William Platt. The man was an able member of the crew, pulled his weight and minded the quartermaster as far as John could see. But today he'd wanted to cuff the bastard and haul him out of the galley by his ear. He stole a glance at Brigit, who'd taken up her position filling the men's mugs with beer again.

If he wanted to remember a time when he'd been this territorial with a woman he'd have to go back to his earliest days at sea, which seemed to him a lifetime ago. Still a whelp of a lad, barely old enough to be called a man, he'd imagined, like a fool, a girl would wait for him all the long months while he sailed. He'd learned that lesson quickly enough, and it had been 'pay for affection' from then on out. Best not to become too fond.

Today, though, he watched with interest as pockets of quiet welled up amid the crew's usual raucous meal time banter while they stood in line for their food. Eyes would flit to the maid, and then back to him, and one deckhand would bend to another's ear and mumble something low and inaudible.

Yes, Platt had spread the word indeed. There would be some stir that not only did the cook not intend to share his unexpected bounty, but that John Bone, usually far less enthusiastic about women than the younger members of the crew, was taking this much of an interest at all.

He dished out several more servings of porridge, greeting the crew as he went.

"Mr George. Winters. Mr Osbourne, Mr Grey. And where's Hezekiah? Isn't he on first watch today?"

"Ha! Don't worry about me, Mr Bone!" The asked-after bosun's voice boomed from the stair as he entered the galley. "You know I won't be missing a meal!"

Yes, this part of his day was as it had been for years. But other parts?

The maid had a small smile for him when he looked her way and he felt a different sort of hunger churn inside him. The idea of Platt laying hands on her had made him miserable, but worse was the idea of her allowing it. The deckhand was a good many years younger than he was, surely more pleasing to the eye for a woman her age.

He'd been so relieved to hear she'd been about to crack him over the head for his troubles. Still, he shouldn't presume her acceptance of his kisses for a night and her calling his name meant she'd given herself over to him and him alone. There was an entire crew of men here, most younger than he, and none missing part of a limb.

For God's sake, John, be easy. None of the men have laid a hand on her, and ye haven't seen her looking at any of them as though she'd want it.

The captain, he suspected, wasn't having any of these sorts of problems with that blonde widow of his. Not if any of the rumours he'd already heard held any water. He sighed to himself. Men on a ship were worse gossips than any circle of wives ever was.

John straightened himself, stretching his back. The line of men was thinning at last. Soon enough he'd have Brigit O'Creagh to himself again, though what sort of promise that held he wasn't yet sure.

Brigit was ready to admit she'd rather liked Bone coming to her defence against the crude advances of the far-too-sure-of-himself Platt, whether she'd truly needed his help or not.

She spooned down her porridge in great mouthfuls, ignoring its bland taste in the wake of the robust appetite she'd built up from the morning's work. Bone stood at the cutting block, scratching away at a piece of parchment with a nubby quill he'd produced from one of the cabinets opposite the stove.

"What are you writing?" she asked, moving to wash her now empty bowl.

"List of what we need at Nassau," he said, appearing to review whatever it was he'd written.

It was some small surprise to see him writing, and she decided to ask him sometime who had taught him. Brigit certainly couldn't write, at least no more than her own name, which her mother had taken pains to see her learn.

She watched his thick fingers fold the paper in two before he turned back to the same cabinet to lock list, quill, and inkwell inside with a small key on a thin leather cord he brought out from inside his shirt. The key reminded her of something Platt had said, and now that she was no longer distracted by having to thwart his attentions, her curiosity reawakened.

"Mr Bone," she said, "may I ask you a question?"

"That depends, lass"—he grinned over at her—"if I answer right, will I have another of those kisses from ye?"

Brigit gave him a look of amusement, but took his tease as permission. "Earlier, Mr Platt said something about Mrs Collingwood being locked up in the captain's room, and that he didn't want to 'share' with the rest of the crew. Is … sharing … with the crew … is that what usually happens?" The end of her question came out as more of a quiet squeak than she'd intended and she silently cursed herself for sounding so afraid.

You're right to be afraid. What do you think you could do if a ship full of criminals was determined to have a go? Run away?

"Well," he said, appearing to take her seriously, "it's not as if we have women on the ship at all regular-like for a man to know *what* 'usually' happens. In fact, I can't think of *any* before the widow and yerself."

He pulled off the heavy apron he'd worn to serve the meal, hanging it on a peg that jutted from the wall near the pantry door. She pressed him, sure she needed an answer but unsure how to ask.

"It was a welcome thing for you to chase Platt above decks today, Mr Bone, but … will I … I mean, does your word carry weight? The other men, will they … will I be expected to …?"

"They'll listen if they want to eat!" He laughed, tugging at the twin braids that fell over his chest. "No, Brigit, I suspect Mr Platt was merely trying his luck this morning. Leave a fine piece of temptation out where men can find it and that's what happens."

Brigit chafed a bit as she bent to stack the unused plates back beneath the cutting block. No man had reason to be calling her a fine piece of anything. It was one thing to enjoy the attention she was receiving from this cook, but quite another to start imagining she was anything other than the first available female to be thrown in amongst a deprived group of men.

Well, second available female.

"Do you think the widow is … is being treated well?" She couldn't help but be at least moderately concerned. The widow likely never had to deal with men of this ilk before their current unplanned adventure. Haughty and stiff though the woman was, she didn't deserve to be used badly.

"Oh, I don't think she'll be hurt," he replied, eyes focused somewhere distant as though he looked elsewhere for a proper way to answer her question. "The captain has a reputation, but I don't imagine he'll do anything yer widow doesn't already want done."

Now *that* was a cryptic way to put it. And Black Edmund, captain of *The Devil's Luck did* have a reputation, though more for merciless looting of ships than anything to do with women. Still …

"Beside all that," Bone said, breaking into her thoughts, "I don't think Mr Till would let her come to any harm. He'll make sure the captain keeps his head about him." It seemed he meant this to be reassuring, but it only confused her further.

"Who's Mr Till, then?"

"Quartermaster."

"Oh. But how will *he* know what the captain and Mrs Collingwood get up to?" She moved to gather up some of the remaining pieces of ship's biscuit and made to return them to their bin in the pantry. Bone took up what was left and followed along behind her.

"Ah. Well." He cleared his throat. "Captain Blackburn and Mr Till are like brothers. They share everything."

Brigit nearly dropped her armful of the hard bread when her mind put together what the cook was trying to explain.

"You mean they …? I mean … *both* of them?" Her

mouth hung partly open as she put away the hard rations of bread, one by one, looking back at Bone for confirmation.

"Probably." His eyes didn't meet hers, and he looked, oddly enough, embarrassed to be telling her this. She couldn't keep her thoughts to herself.

"That poor woman! I don't think she has any idea what to do with *one* man, let alone two."

Some small piece of something had worked its way into her slipper, and Brigit leaned against a tall stack of several bags of what was probably grain to stand on one foot and pull off the shoe opposite to shake it loose.

"Well I wasn't there, lass, but I did hear from some of the men who were on watch last night and I don't think that'll be a problem." He chuckled as he put the last of his own share of the tack away. She wiggled her shoe back on and looked up at him.

"What makes you say that?"

He turned a merry eye her way. "Some of the crew who passed by the door to the stateroom heard yer widow, ah … 'enjoying' Mr Till and the captain's company, if ye will?" He grinned at this, pleased with his turn of phrase. "Said she was making a fine lot of noise, too. Though I don't think she sounded at all as lovely as ye did last night, pretty girl."

Bone had a conspiratorial wink for her at this, but Brigit had heard enough. She folded her arms across her chest and met his eye.

I'll not be mocked.

"Don't call me that, John Bone. I'm no man's 'pretty girl', and you know it."

He looked crestfallen, and for a moment she winced at her own harshness.

"I'm sorry, Mrs O'Creagh. I thought we—"

"No!" She wouldn't play these games. "I'm happy for us to … to have our fun down here, Mr Bone. You seem an honourable man, and I don't know that I expected as much from a pirate, but I'll have an end to all the 'pretty' and 'lovely', if you please. I know what I am, and I know what I'm not."

His face grew dark at her words, and he drew himself up, taking a step towards her. Not the reaction she'd been expecting. She flattened herself against the sacks of grain.

"What do ye mean, ye know what ye are?" His voice was low now, menacing. Brigit stood her ground.

"Don't play with me, Mr Bone. A woman doesn't have a face that looks like mine without being told about it. It's a wonder the crew had any appetite at all after my serving them."

For a man his size, he certainly could move. In a breath he was on her, pinning her against the stack of sacks. Blue eyes flashed and he gripped her chin between thumb and forefinger, brows drawn down in anger as he towered over her.

"Don't ye ever—*ever!*—let me hear ye speak of yerself that way again!" His words came in a growl. She'd not seen temper like this yet from the man, and it made her want to cower. His eyes searched hers for an excruciating moment and Brigit felt something inside herself break.

"John, I—"

"Which one of us is perfect, Brigit?" He rushed to cut her off, giving his peg a solid thump against the deck to make his point.

In the space of a breath she went from cynical to welling with tears. The man was missing a *leg*, and she'd been grumbling about her looks. She couldn't meet his eyes and her gaze fell to the grim line of his mouth, his beard. His body softened against hers then and he released her chin, though he still kept her trapped between him and the grain. She shifted on her feet, preparing to say something, anything, when he spoke again, less angry this time, but still terribly serious.

"Now you listen to *me*, Brigit O'Creagh. *I* know what ye are, as well. You're a bright young woman who wasn't supposed to board a pirate ship. Ye were handed over to a man ye didn't know, a lame cook who's old enough to know better himself, and ye smiled at him all the same."

She *really* couldn't look at him now, though her hands moved of their own accord to grip fistfuls of his shirt in an effort to steel herself against the onslaught of unfamiliar emotions his words were bringing.

"And not only did ye smile," he continued, making her face heat up even more, "ye made his entire day bright. The minute ye fell down the stairs and I caught ye, Brigit, I was already a lost cause. And now this morning I'm ready to knock another man on his arse for his even thinking he can have ye. Because *I* want ye. So you'll be called 'pretty girl' and 'lass' and whatever other names I can think of, and I'll hear no more fuss over it!"

Not even half a heartbeat passed after she met his eyes again before they'd seized one another up in a furious, desperate kiss. His two hands were on either side of her face and she clutched at his shoulders, devouring in a fever the sincere want this man offered; the one thing she'd never, ever had.

Their tongues spoke silent, urgent volumes into each other.

A nip of teeth at a lower lip.

I want this.

A deep, curling sweep of a tongue, one across the other.

Do you see what this does to me?

A greedy pull of lips and a quiet groan.

I need you. Can you feel it?

Somewhere in the delirium of acceptance, his kisses had trailed down her chin and over her jaw. His mouth pulled at her ear and lapped at her throat, and she clung to him, even as his arms crushed them together at the waist.

Bone stilled his consumption of her with his face buried in her neck and merely held her to him, breath coming hot against her collar bone. She could feel his chest expanding with the labour of his lungs in the dim quiet of the pantry, and she brought her arms around his neck, fingertips painting soft strokes over the back of his shaven head as they stood this way, immersed in simple, shared warmth for a time.

The still hum of desire in the room and the press of their bodies was making Brigit restless now. Without thought, her hips shifted, rolling against the cook. Through her skirts and petticoats she felt him, hard as stone, and he mumbled a low curse when the firm rise of her mound nudged at him through the fabric.

When he drew back to look at her then, the raw need in his eyes all but set the air in the room on fire. Something inside her chest felt as though it was being crushed in a tight grip. Brigit knew she wanted far more than his mouth on her today. And for more days than today.

What is this? These feelings?

A delicious vibration of fear trilled up her spine, but not for anything John Bone might do to her body. No, of that she wasn't afraid at all.

As though someone brave and self-assured had taken command of her body, Brigit shifted her bottom up onto the top of the pile of grain bags and fisted her hand into the centre of Bone's shirt, pulling him towards her even as she leaned back to support her own weight with her other arm.

She moved her knees wide apart and curled her feet around the back of his thighs as he stepped into the brazen space she'd made for him. Their eyes remained locked as Brigit made plain with the language of her body how very ready she was. He leaned in to kiss her again, and some inner voice told her there ought to be words. She needed to tell him.

"John," she said, stopping him before he could close the last of the distance to her lips.

"Brigit." His words came at a rasp, eyes on her mouth, loathe to delay what they both so obviously wanted.

Liquid tension burned between her thighs, and she wanted him to know it. To hear what he'd done to her.

Brigit reached back through years of living in the less desirable parts of a city, of hearing rough men speak using language she wasn't supposed to know. She found the most shocking, wanton thing she could think to say to him and said it, nearly shattering in disbelief at the sound of the words on her own tongue.

"I want you to fuck me."

The sharp intake of breath from the man was almost a gasp at hearing her say such a thing. He wedged the firm heat of his erection tighter between them, almost bruising the splayed flesh of her sex, even beneath the layers of skirt and shift.

"Is that what ye want, Brigit?" he asked, his tone quiet and dangerous, the question spilling into her open mouth as he ground himself against her. "Ye want me to fuck ye?"

His hands were at the fabric of her skirts, gathering it up as he spoke. They were toying with one another now, the teasing words mere ornament. The maid and the cook had agreed upon their destination long ago.

"No, I don't want it," she said, slipping nimble fingers to the fastenings of his breeches, not to be outdone. "I need it."

He sprang free with a growl at her words and she had her hand on him for the first time, just as he got the last of her hemline tucked up to her waist. The air in the pantry curled over her skin, drawing her attention to just how wet she'd become.

And him! She could hardly circle her fingers around his girth, but she plied him with appreciative strokes all the same, pleased to hear him hiss through clenched teeth at the slide of a soft hand over his throbbing heat. Brigit tugged him closer and he followed her lead, moving his hips in to rest the length of his cock over the slick temptation she offered.

"What is it ye need now?" he teased, sliding himself along her entrance, nudging the plump tip against her aching little nub. It seemed he enjoyed her filthy mouth as much as she'd hoped, and now he wanted to play.

I can play.

"I need your cock inside me, John," she said, watching his jaw tighten in response to her bawdy suggestion. Brigit felt him twitch against her and she tilted her hips, working to tempt him into forfeit. "I want you to fuck me," she repeated, growing bold.

Her words proved too much for the cook and she melted in relief when she felt the blunt velvet of him burrowing into her, though only a fraction of the way, not all of him as she wanted.

"Is this what ye want, pretty girl?" He tormented her with only a shallow push in and out, stretching her entrance but never sheathing himself, and more, she didn't wince at his endearment now. The look on his face, the pain of careful restraint, told her he might actually mean what he said. It was maddening, and her feet pressed at his backside, trying to urge him forward. It appeared she would need to play along.

"Yes, John, please!" She didn't even need to feign desperation. He needed to stop toying with her and—

"Oh!"

She was full.

More than full. Stretched, overflowing.

"John!"

"Christ, Brigit!" He held himself still, thumping into the luxury of her core.

With her weight on one arm, she slid her other palm up beneath his shirt. She needed to touch him. Her fingers splayed over his chest, passing over the warm expanse of muscle there, the dusting of hair, the hard line of his collarbone. The swollen lips between her thighs kissed up against the seat of his shaft and something inside her sucked at him, begging for what she wanted.

He gave it to her.

It was slow at first. Excruciating. She felt every slick,

hard inch of him draw out and then deliberately revisit each nook and ridge inside her on the tortuous way back in. Again he did this. And again. The man had the patience of a mountain and she didn't know whether to call this treatment cruel or indescribably perfect.

She found herself writhing under him, urging him to end the torment and take her, to let go and assault her with his cock the way she wanted. The whining noises she was making brought a low chuckle from the man between her legs and he buried himself to the hilt in response, stopping his movement entirely.

"Oh please!" she whimpered, squirming.

How can he be so calm?

His hand came up and with a few sharp tugs like he'd done the night before, he brought the sleeves of her dress away from her shoulders and the stiff wrap of her stays lower around her ribs. Her breasts jutted free now, the bones of the garment pressing them upward, nipples tight and dark, as eager as the rest of her for John Bone's attention.

Back arched and still completely within her, he brought his face to his new prize and took one of the tense little buds into his mouth. He suckled at her, slow and sweet, as though he meant to heal a wound with the pull of his lips and teeth. Her head lolled back as she gave over to whatever he wanted to do.

Moments or hours later, she didn't know which, he shifted over to the neglected tip on the other side, and with that began to move his hips again. Brigit nearly fell apart.

Her hand was on the back of his neck, cradling his head as he bent to his task, and her heels were pressing into the small of his back, as if she needed to make it any clearer what she wanted. Somewhere in the lusty haze of tangling limbs, one of her slippers had fallen off.

He was pushing into her now at a more satisfying pace, some of his earlier restraint wearing thin. Brigit arched into his movements, leaning back further to take in more of him. Her breast bounced away from his mouth in a wet pop once she'd stretched beyond his reach, and with that distraction ended he stood up straighter and brought his hands to her hips. With the delicious press of his thumbs at the crease where her widely parted thighs met her hips, Bone found leverage and began at last do what she'd asked. He began to fuck her.

She watched him bite at his lower lip in concentration as the working muscles of his thighs and backside slapped his body against her greedy pussy. More, she delighted in his eyes on her tits as they bounced with the rhythm of his thrusts. She brought her own hands up and cupped them, tugging at the nipples, squeezing them high and together for his enjoyment. The strained groan she got in response told her she'd guessed correctly what a man would like to see.

His pumping had taken on a measure of ferocity now, and she had no idea how he was managing to keep up such a forceful pace with his leg as it was. There was no time for thoughts like those, however. Brigit felt her own bottom flexing as she pushed herself back against the driving of his cock, working up a promising friction between her most sensitive pearl of flesh and the curling nest of hair at the base of his shaft.

Oh yes, this was good. Spinning flashes of pleasure began to jar up from the place he grazed at her, bursting like flowers of lightning over her belly. If only she could just tilt herself so—

"John, I'm—aughhh!"

Brigit came around him with a wild cry before she could even tell him what was happening, though doubtless he could tell. Her walls spasmed and clutched at the driving length of him, and the building tightness in her loins exploded and danced around the rigid flesh of what she realised might be her first real lover.

The pulses of release wouldn't stop, and when he angled his hips to spear at her from an even shallower angle, the head of his cock found some new node of pleasure to kiss at the bottom of each thrust. Her delight shifted into another key altogether.

She began to laugh as the fluttering surged out around him again, and nearly wept when the release went on and on. A new rush of moisture spilled from her body and she felt him tense and begin to drive into her with a fury, the signal given that he could now have his pleasure, as well.

He brought himself inside with deep, vicious strokes, and her thighs parted wide, welcoming his final push for satisfaction.

Brigit felt him grow impossibly hard, his movements jerky and erratic for a wild disconnected moment. Then his hips flew back leaving her suddenly vacant, humming.

The cook growled out a curse and she looked down in time to see the fat pink head of his cock pushing through his fist. His body seized up and a jet of white, hot completion arced over her lips to splatter and pool above her mound. A second spurt followed and then a third, which didn't quite make it onto her swollen pussy, and these he accompanied with further satisfied bits of profanity.

She lay there limp and sated, and Bone steadied himself with one palm on the bulkhead above her, his chest heaving, and throat moving to wet itself again. What this said of her she didn't know, but Brigit had never felt more accomplished in all her life.

When his eyes opened again and found hers she couldn't keep a smile from splitting her face. He grinned back and let out a short rumbling laugh as they both worked to catch their breath.

Several more weeks to Nassau? I don't know if that will be enough time at all.

Brigit held her skirts up out of the way and teased her new lover with a knowing smirk.

"I think we've a bit of a mess on our hands, Mr Bone."

"I think we do," he answered with a serious nod but a tone that shared her jest.

Oh yes, several weeks would be just a tease. She wanted this pirate for much longer than that.

The second night she shared his bed came earlier than the first. Once they'd served the evening meal and tidied the galley for the next day, they were both far too weary on their feet to do anything else. The afternoon's exertions at the back of the pantry proved enough to send them to his bunk early. That meant no sneaking in while the bulk of the crew was already asleep.

He still had his back to the open space of the hold, but after a day of Platt's tongue-wagging—as he'd directed, to be sure—quite a few of the men who made their way in to find their hammocks had lewd taunts for John and his new bed mate.

"Has he let ye see where he stores the meat then, girl?"

"What o' those tits? Will there be fresh milk for breakfast?"

"You shown her you still have *two* good legs, Bone?"

Brigit lay facing him tonight and her hand went to cover her open mouth at the jabs of the sailors. Her wide eyes told him she was stifling laughter, though. He shook his head and rolled his eyes with a smirk. This was how men spoke, and the appearance of one young maid wasn't likely to change it. At least she wasn't scowling.

He took the hand she held to her lips and caught the pads of her fingers up between his teeth, nipping at her. She wriggled closer to him in the dim light and he stole an arm around her waist.

For some unbelievable amount of time they did nothing more than stare at each other, each marvelling in their own way at the day's developments. John felt like some fool boy who'd never been hip to hip with a woman. As though it were still 1696 and he'd explode after a few quick thrusts or turn all red and flustered after seeing a pair of tits.

Brigit's fingertips flirted over his mouth and the side of his face, moved to have a playful tug at the braids of his beard. He couldn't help but smile at her. She said nothing but her hand moved over his shoulder, and then down to squeeze at his arm, as though confirming for herself he was real.

The light touches were somehow waking his cock back up, if it could be believed after his wild spending earlier. It throbbed to show its readiness again as she leaned in to brush a light kiss over his lips. There was no tongue, it wasn't fiery or demanding, just a display of her newfound comfort in his presence. Yes, all sorts of dormant notions had been flickering back to life since Blackburn had flung this girl into his care yesterday.

John circled his fingers around her wrist and brought her hand down between them, settling it on his hardness and learning a new way to raise her brows higher.

"Do ye see what ye do to me, lass?" he whispered, low enough that none of the settling men in the hold might hear.

She chewed at her lip and gripped him through his breeches, tucking herself closer against his body. Her slight nod and the question on her face drove a low chuckle out of him, though.

She wants to know if ye expect her to do anything about it. Can ye imagine? Here in the hold, half the crew milling around?

"No, no," he assured her with a smile, barely audible. Pulling her hand back to his waist, he shifted more to his comfort. "Sleep, lass."

With a final kiss, she relaxed against him, tucking her head under his chin. The maid smelled far better than a cabin full of men and he concentrated on telling his prick to go to sleep, as well.

John mused to himself that he might just be able to convince her to remain with him after Nassau, if fate allowed him a few more days like today. The question was, would Captain Blackburn permit *either* of the two new women to remain aboard? The good thing about being cook, though, was that a body heard all of a ship's gossip. He'd simply keep his ears open and listen for which way the wind blew. If the captain wanted to put the widow ashore, perhaps John could make a case for keeping Brigit on as help.

She made some small sound and nuzzled her face into his throat. Yes. It seemed there was far more work to be done around the galley of *The Devil's Luck* of late. Not a man could be spared. Or woman. A young one. From Cork.

He slept.

Chapter 3

Blades and Madness

"A taste for adventure is by no means a masculine monopoly."
— Lloyd Alexander

"Now and then we had a hope that if we lived and were good, God would permit us to be pirates."
— Mark Twain, *Life on the Mississippi*

The thread drew taut again as she raised the needle above the line of her eyes. Brigit tugged at it to make the stitch tight before jabbing through the heavy fabric to start another. Instead of having her help him with the meal today, Bone had set her to sewing pudding bags. She was on her third of the four he wanted.

She sat on a low stool, the same one the cook had used that first night when he pulled up to feast between her thighs, doing the work he was relieved to give over, under the claim that his fingers were always too large and clumsy for proper needlework. They hadn't seemed clumsy when they—

"Ow!"

Bone's head swivelled to see what her noise-making was about. "Can I not trust ye to be alone with a pudding bag without hurting yerself, lass?" His tone teased, but his features did hold a hair of concern as he slipped into the pantry.

"No," she called after him, pulling the fingertip out of her mouth, "It seems you can't. Perhaps I've pricked my finger to keep myself awake."

That was certainly true enough, with all the daydreaming she'd been doing. Brigit assessed the tiny wound and, as it appeared to be no longer bleeding, went back to sewing the sides of the bag together.

"Whose prick are ye fingering now?" he asked with a grin as he emerged from the storage room with an armful of small jars.

"Beast." She shook her head at him and returned his smirk. Brigit was growing to enjoy the salty familiarity that had arisen between her and this cook.

Familiar, and yet …

Yes, she thought as she drew the line of stitches along, here was a man who made intimate jests with her, who'd seen more of her body than any one other man, and here she sat knowing hardly anything about him. Perhaps he could be persuaded to talk a bit more today.

And what do you want to know of him? He may not want to be peppered with questions, girl.

Brigit watched Bone busy himself about the galley. By most respectable standards he was a bit of a knave, if one considered the way he'd approached her two days ago. She hadn't pushed him away though, or spurned his advances, and he *had* been more than a little interested in her pleasure as well as his own. Even before his own, if she considered the order of events.

And yet surrounding the relative safety of the galley was a ship full of cutthroats. *The Devil's Luck* was well known to be crewed by merciless men, the sort who'd put a man over the side for the weight of a purse. Sailors who had no place in a proper navy. But here was John Bone who seemed only kind; a man who fed scraps to a cat, for pity's sake. What was *he* doing among such men?

There, and now you have it.

"Mr Bone," she said, setting down the completed third bag and taking up material for the fourth, "how did you come to sail aboard *The Devil's Luck*?"

"Well now," he said, nudging about in the belly of the stove with a poker, "Isn't *that* a question?"

Brigit watched as he straightened himself, leaning the poker against the wall of the hull. He wiped at his hands while he appeared to gather his answer.

"I've been with Captain Blackburn from the beginning. It has to have been … oh, some twelve, fourteen years now? It's hard to remember. Maybe longer."

"Have you always been the cook?" She took up the needle again now that she'd drawn him into a conversation.

"Oh no, that didn't happen until I lost the leg. That was some seven years ago."

Brigit considered this as her eyes were back on her work. For a time, before he was down here feeding sailors, Bone was a regular part of the crew. He'd probably taken lives the same as anyone else aboard the ship. She didn't know yet what she thought of this. How was he different from any other man who followed his captain's orders? What made a man a murderer?

"Who was Cook before?" she asked instead, keeping her questions to topics less likely to be upsetting. "What happened to him?"

Bone grunted, leaning against the pantry door frame, his favourite place to stand and take the weight off his leg, it seemed. "Heh. Captain didn't much care for him. When he saw I wouldn't be keeping my leg, he gave the galley over to me, instead."

"But did he …?"

A bark of laughter erupted from the bald man across the kitchen when he saw her wide-eyed look. "No, no!

Nothing like that. Mr Till and the captain ended his contract and put him ashore in Kingston. Captain Blackburn isn't a madman, Mrs O'Creagh. He doesn't go about killing men for sport, though I'd wager you've heard otherwise."

She eyed him for a moment before looking back to the needle. He hadn't lied to her so far, but he was right about what she'd heard. Black Edmund *did* have a reputation for doing a great many horrible things without remorse. Still, Bone didn't seem the sort to sail under the command of someone so devoid of humanity.

"And before this ship?" Brigit wanted more; wanted to know all he would tell her. "That is, how did you come to be here?"

"Ah, another ship, another captain," he said, waving her off with a gesture of his hand. The curl of his lip at the end of his sentence spoke volumes and she pressed him in her curiosity.

"This other captain … was the reason you're on this ship now instead of that one?"

"Nothing makes it past ye, does it, pretty girl?" He favoured her with a wry grin as he folded his arms over his chest. "Aye, Captain Trask was meant to do nothing else but lead a crew of scoundrels. Born on Newgate steps he was, and the perfect man for this life." Bone shook his head at some distant memory she couldn't see.

"Why did you leave his ship, then?" The needle rose and fell with her questions, and Brigit shifted on the stool. Her task was keeping her from giving full attention to his answers, and she was eager to have done with it.

"Oh, he was an able enough captain, I suppose." The cook sighed as he pulled the braids of his beard through his fingers, eyes on the ceiling. "And I was barely a man when I joined his crew, no older than sixteen. I hadn't learnt the difference yet. He was fair with the crew and we always got our even shares; purses were always full. But a body comes to see, after a time, that there's nothing to be done for some men. They'll nettle ye, even to look at them, and Trask began to devil me just so."

"What do you mean, 'devil you'?" The last of her words came out mangled as she reached the end of her sewing and bit the thread in two. It was crude, but she had no shears or knife on hand.

"Well, now," he said, "some of the crew weren't bothered by his ways, but they made *me* uneasy. He'd empty his own purse too quickly when we went ashore, give ye a different answer each time you'd ask him a question. The man shifted like the wind and there was no telling from one day to the next what sort of temper he'd be in. The sea is shifty enough, and I came to see I no longer wanted to sail under a man who couldn't stand fast against it."

Bone almost seemed bored with the telling of his own story, and his eyes were elsewhere, unfocused. Brigit was not bored at all. She watched him roll his head from one side to the other, eyes shut and creases coming at the bridge of his nose as he pulled through the pleasant ache of stretching the muscles in his neck. She found herself well pleased with the way the linen of his shirt drew tight over the broad mass of his shoulders as he did this, and was struck with the memory of her leg draped over one of them while he made her squirm with his tongue.

Damn me if I don't want to make him do the same.

Brigit cleared her throat.

"So you'd rather have certainty?" She goaded him now as her mood turned a sharp corner. "I thought you pirates wanted adventure?"

"Not this pirate!" He laughed, his gaze snapping back to her, treating her to the grin that made her want to bury her face in his chest. "At least not nearly as much as Captain Trask was giving me. I'd like to know I've a place to rest my head and fill my belly. As much as a man *can* know in this life. And I wouldn't leave it now. The sea is my home." He finished with a sweeping gesture that took in the surrounding cabin, meaning the ship and, more broadly, the sea. Her thoughts were barely on his words now, though.

She felt her thighs slip, wet against one another, as she bent to the side to gather up the bags she'd sewn. A lush tumble of thoughts fell on her like she'd opened a door to an overstuffed linen closet. There were things. Things men had asked for that Brigit O'Creagh knew to do. Things that would have him cursing or calling her name or both. She very much wanted to show this man what she knew.

But how will you ask to do such a thing? Can you even say the words?

Perhaps she could entice him into meeting her halfway.

Yes. It worked two days ago and you weren't even trying.

Brigit came to her feet, some shred of a plan in mind, determined to see John Bone learn to receive as well as he gave. The sea was his home, was it? It seemed to her that for a home, it was missing some of the comforts a man should have.

They won't be missing for long.

She smiled to herself.

"And does Black E—, I mean, *Captain* Blackburn, is he more … steadfast?" She corrected herself on the captain's name as she stood, her tone light and teasing. It endeared her to him further that she bothered to respect the man's dislike of his nickname, even though he suspected her opinions of Blackburn were sceptical at best. Here was a woman who learned quickly.

"He is that, lass, he is that," He watched her move to the near side of the cutting block as he finished his thoughts aloud. "You'll never see him half seas over with the crew or changing his mind about the course when we're three weeks from port. No, our captain may not be jolly like the bosun or have pretty words to say like Mr Adams, but you'll always know where ye stand with him, and that suits me just fine."

Something had shifted in her movements while he spoke, and part of him that had been asleep moments ago had come awake with the change. Her hips rolled in some deliberate way as she came to stand with her back to him, using the waist-high surface to fold the finished bags.

"*You* seem to be full of pretty words, John Bone," she said over her shoulder, bending forward to rest her elbows and forearms atop the block. "Taking galley maids for a look at the sunrise … putting fine notions in their ears." The maid twisted a mischievous smile back at him, all but waggling that plump backside of hers in his direction, and he nearly forgot the rest of the conversation. Shades of some of his first lusty thoughts of her came flitting back.

… *bent at the middle over the edge of the cutting block, skirts up over her round bottom* …

He swallowed, wetting his throat.

"Are ye tempting me, girl?" he asked, aiming to keep his voice level.

"What if I am?" The arch of her brow and tilt of her jaw told him all he needed to know. In a breath he was behind her, hands at her hips, pulling the inviting backside with a bounce against his growing arousal.

"So help me, Brigit …" he ground out between clenched teeth. He was too sensible a man to be coming undone this way, his mind fogging over with lust at the sight, the sound of this woman.

I think this one may be different, John.

Without warning, she slid in his grasp and turned to face him, twining her arms about his waist and staring up to meet his eyes with cheekily feigned innocence as she pressed herself to him.

"Help you do what?"

Ohhh, this one.

He seized up her mouth in the kiss her expression all but begged for, stopping to admonish her as he went.

"I've got a bloody … kitchen to run." Between hungry sounds he scolded her, and she teased him back with nips of her teeth and the subtle clawing of nails at his back. "I can't spend … all day with … my prick fighting the inside of my breeches."

Her hands had wandered down to his backside during their bout of needy kisses, fingers kneading at the muscle there, causing him an odd flare of pride that this young maid could want him enough to touch him so. Before there was time for further thought, however, one of those hands was making its way over his hip and …

He hissed and it trailed off into a groan. Brigit had him in a firm grip and gave a squeeze to get his attention. She had it.

"You won't have to spend *all* day," she said, sliding her curled fingers along his aching length.

Her voice had taken on a low, throaty tone he hadn't thought her capable of, and he throbbed against her touch, grabbing up his own handfuls of bottom, crushing her teasing hand between them.

"It's not right to toy with a man, Mrs O'Creagh." The words rasped directly into her mouth. She still sought to heighten his desire with a scattering of urgent kisses, even as he spoke.

"Who's toying, then?" She drew back and looked at him, eyes serious but a faint smile curling her lips. There was movement at his waist, and her fingers slid, travelling under the edge of his breeches. Like a much younger man, his heart hammered in his chest by the time Brigit spoke again. "What was it you said to me? 'Let's see to you, shall we?' Well? Let's."

Flesh made contact with flesh and fire danced over his skin. A palm brushed over the joining of leg to hip, making him jerk and take in a sharp breath. And then her hand was on him, cool fingers against the heat of his shaft, slipping towards the base while her other hand worked fastenings apart.

With a shift and a tug, he was free, standing out in the open air. Brigit grinned at him as though *she* might be the one with the luck, and not the devil the ship was named for. She held his gaze with a challenge in those green eyes of hers and slid to her knees.

Oh, save me. I'm done for.

A feminine hand stroked at his length, priming him while he stood. He stared down in mute disbelief. She cast an approving eye over the jutting, eager cock in her grip, and he felt himself twitch and swell at the idea of her doing this out of want and not obligation.

"Where shall we start, Mr Bone?" she asked, aiming him at the ceiling with her fist as she swept the pad of her thumb over the sensitive skin just beneath the flare at the end of his shaft.

He looked down, dumb, shaking his head, too enthralled with the sight of her to form words. She knelt before him, the swell of her breasts labouring over her neckline, the pretty bow of her mouth curved in a smile. A mirage, most men would say, on a ship like this.

"Perhaps from the bottom?" she suggested, voice sweet as she ignored the stiff flesh in her hand and instead gently took the loose skin of his balls into her mouth.

This was a horrible time to be missing part of a leg: it was hard enough for a man to stand on *two* buckling knees. Lips made their delicate pull at his most tender flesh and he shored himself up with all his might. The last thing he needed was to fall before she—

A groan rose up from his throat. She'd drawn one of his testicles fully into her mouth and began to suckle, rolling it around over her tongue.

"Brigit! What are ye—"

Its twin received the same treatment and now her fingers wrapped around his girth, stroking, pulling. He had to put a hand to the cutting block behind her to steady himself.

Her attention had moved elsewhere, though, and now she was dragging her tongue in a deliberate, slow rasp along the lower side of his cock. He made the mistake of opening his eyes then, only to meet her gaze just as the stout, pink head was flattening her tongue as it hovered in wait over her open mouth.

For a moment, he was suspended in time. Wide green eyes offered up such a gift to him, the likes of which he'd never imagined when the captain had given her over to his employ a mere two days ago. He'd expected at worst a nuisance, and at best something nice to look at. And now?

Brigit paused in her actions, warm breath curling over his skin in a wicked little tease as she held the end of him between parted lips, not yet closing in around his eager, swollen prick. His hips gave a subtle thrust of anticipation and her eyes twinkled up at him.

"Brigit …"

"Mmm?" Wet warmth sank in around him as she ceased her games. Lips and tongue drew him in, greedy, accepting. The entire world had shrunk to include only him and this maid on her knees. Her mouth pulled at his cock, suckling in heady, unashamed appreciation. She made the act look like the greatest joy a woman could receive. Her eyes were closed, and small, languid sounds of satisfaction hummed through his flesh.

As he stood there, trying to remain upright under her luxurious assault, she paused in the attention she was lavishing over him to pull back, her eye seeming to take his measure. She appeared to make some decision and then engulfed him again.

This time, though, her movements were more careful. She slid farther down the length of him now, and halted her progress at intervals as she went, adjusting her lips and tongue along the way. He watched, speechless as, with ginger movements, she took more and more of him into her mouth until the tip of her nose came to meet the curls at his base.

Brigit released a moan and a small sigh, her goal achieved, and simply held her position for a time. Her eyes remained closed and the wet contours of her tongue and palate shifted around him. He couldn't stop himself from throbbing, wedged down her throat as he was, and the sudden pulse made her draw back in a rush to gasp, yanking him free into the cool air.

His pretty maid was undeterred though, and gripped him again, taking aim with his shaft and plunging him once more between her lips. This time she was able to take all of him with more ease, and arrived in no time at the root of his need. She shifted her knees closer to him with a muffled sound of triumph, and her fingers slid up over his thighs, thumbs coming to curl in just at the bones of his hips. She rolled her eyes up to him again, and what she asked for with her gaze was beyond belief.

"Ye … want me to …?"

A slow nod from the lovely creature on her knees before him, this woman who wanted to please him but couldn't answer aloud because she'd buried his cock between her jaws. The pads of her fingers gave a light squeeze of confirmation, sinking into the meat of his hips. Those eyes wanted nothing but to see him satisfied.

He reached down and drew his thumb across her brow, over her cheekbone, along the taut line of her upper lip where it wrapped around him. She was completely still and patient, waiting for him to decide to do it.

This is a dream. I'll wake from this, won't I?

His fingers combed back into her hair along the side of her face, curling in to grip a loose handful near the scalp. With a slight movement of hips, he brought himself out of her mouth before making a tentative nudge back into the hot, wet promise she offered. Tightly checking his urge to plunge himself home again and again, John watched the expression on her face for any sign this wasn't her intent.

God, but it must be. If I'm to stop now …

"Is this what you're after?" he growled, bumping against the roof of her mouth as he rocked forward a bit, hand still in her hair. "Ye want a man's cock down yer throat?" He pulled out again, tired of nods and suggestive looks, wanting to hear her answer aloud.

"No," she said, eyes dark with need, "I want *your* cock down my throat, John Bone. Now haven't you something to eat for your pretty girl?"

Something clenched in his belly and her words possessed him. He sank in at once to the hilt with an exultant grunt and, having seated himself fully that first time, took up his grip in those dark, honey-coloured locks again and began to pump, feeding everything he had into her open, accepting mouth.

So good. Damn me, but that's good.

Incredibly, her eyes rolled up at this and a soft moan shivered along the firm length of muscle he was working past her lips. John watched her hands fall to her chest as he settled into a steady rhythm. Her fingers delved below the edge of her bodice and in a fluid movement she brought her breasts out over the top, tightened nipples immediately taken up by her own pinching and rolling. The wanton picture she presented made him catch his breath.

His voice came strained now as he pushed further, deeper. "Christ! A man can only … take so much! I—"

Something darkened at the edge of his vision.

His eye jumped away from Brigit to see a pair of feet on the stair, legs, knees.

Fuck!

He jerked back from the maid and her eyes flew open as she reeled at his departure.

"Mr Bone!" came the call from sailor thumping down the steps, "Just the man I've come to see!"

John yanked the tail of his shirt down over his slick, bobbing erection.

"Afternoon, Hawke," he said, gaze darting to the wide-eyed Brigit, still kneeling in front of him. She was frozen in mortified terror. "What say ye?"

The cook nearly collapsed with relief when the younger man stopped halfway down the stair, leaning on his palm against the hull as he answered back.

"Uh ..." Hawke squinted into the galley. "Are you all right, Mr Bone?"

Lord be praised, he can't see her.

The mass of the cutting block was obscuring the maid from Hawke's view, and it seemed, by some stroke of luck, to be hiding his suspiciously askew shirt and breeches, as well. John let out the breath he was holding.

"I'm right as can be, Hawke."

"You sure?" the man asked, "Thought I heard you swearing away when I came through the hatch."

"Ah, well"—he made a quick excuse and a dismissive gesture of his head—"the leg gets to me sometimes, ye know."

There was a tug at his waist. In the half a glance he could spare at the floor, he saw Brigit had moved his breeches aside again and had him in hand. Her eyes sparked with mischief, and she brought a single finger to her lips, signalling him to silence above a sly grin.

She wouldn't dare.

"What brings ye to the galley between meals, Mr Hawke?"

He had to keep the deckhand from coming any further into the room.

"Right," the sailor said, mercifully standing where he was, "Do you dice, Mr Bone?"

Her lips were on him again. His hand was a fist at his side, tension gripping him about the throat. Hawke remained oblivious.

"It's been a ... while, but I've been known to roll the bones a time ... or two. Why?"

She was bobbing her head now, challenging him to hold himself together. Her mouth was so hot, and the way it slid ...

Pray he doesn't notice the way ye can't string a sentence together, John.

"Well then!" He still had no idea. Good. "Mr Grey and Mr Hezekiah have sent me 'round to see if you'll join us for a game after evening meal."

"Grey's purse getting light again, is it?" He managed a laugh, but her tongue was squirming over that damned ridge. John bit at the inside of his cheek to stifle a groan.

"I imagine it is!" The other man chuckled, one hand to the knee that remained on the higher step.

Soft fingertips pulled and massaged at the skin of his scrotum and he covered a grunt of surprise with an abrupt cough.

This woman, I swear …

"Very well, Hawke, tell him I'll be there." The man needed to shove off, already.

Strong suckling from below. He braced himself.

"That maid of yours can come along, if you want." Hawke glanced around the galley. "Is she not here?"

A flickering of tongue darted into the slit at the tip of his cock.

Oh, I'll need to take her over my knee after this!

"She's off to the head."

The sailor grinned, the beak of his nose splitting his face in two. "Heard the two of you were bedded down right cozy-like in that bunk of yours last night." Blond brows tipped up in suggestion.

John shrugged with half a grin of his own. What was there to deny?

A shiver wiggled up his spine.

Was that her teeth?

"That be all, Mr Hawke?"

He *had* to get this man out of here.

The deckhand nodded in the direction of the block. "Throw me a piece of that biscuit, Bone?"

He squinted at the man. Some of the crew would always try for more than their daily portion, but he needed this one gone, and now.

Heaven's sake! Don't bring a thumb into it, girl!

John grabbed a ration of tack from the bin and tossed it to the sailor on the stair, who caught it spinning out of its arc and raised it in an appreciative gesture.

"My thanks, Mr Bone!"

There were light kisses now, along the shaft. She was showing *some* sort of mercy.

"Well tuck it away, Hawke, or the rest will be down here wanting more than their share, as well."

"Right," he said, stuffing the hard round of bread into a pocket. "See you for dice then, Bone." The lanky man made his goodbye over a shoulder as he hoisted himself with his bent knee and ascended through the hatch as quickly as he'd come

His breath came out with a rush of air as soon as he saw the last of Hawke's boots, and a giggle curled up from beneath the tented hem of his shirt. He yanked back the fabric to see green eyes glinting up at him, a hand clapped over her mouth now to hold back laughter. He shook his head.

"Ye find that amusing, do ye?" Her chuckles sputtered out around her fingers in response along with vigorous nodding. "Saucy thing." It was difficult for either one of them to keep a straight face with his prick still jumping in the air for attention.

"I'm sorry, John." Her laughter was uncontainable. "But you *were* brilliant just now. Mr Hawke didn't suspect a thing!"

The playful manner of the woman on her knees was contagious, and there was still the matter of his stiff cock that needed addressing. He fisted his hand into her hair once more, roughly pulling her face close to his arousal.

"If I recall correctly, Mrs O'Creagh, there's someone else who wanted an extra portion before evening meal. Isn't that so?" There was a teasing note of threat in his voice as he used his other hand to guide the healthy pink head back and forth over her lower lip.

"That *is* so, Mr Bone," she said, voice smoky as she gave him an impertinent little lick, lapping up the clear bead of dew that had formed at the end of his raging lust. Her neck was bent up to him, lips slightly parted in anticipation, hands resting on her thighs. His grip at her scalp and the command he took seemed to have increased the rate of her breathing.

"Then finish what ye started, lass, and ye shall have it."

John angled his cock down with his free hand and with those words, sheathed it to the root between her pretty lips.

Her eyes bulged for a moment and she made a startled noise at his thrust, but when he drew back she moaned, eyes closing in bliss, and he knew she wanted him to have this from her as much as he did.

Now.

There were no interruptions this time and he found his stride in mere moments. The ripe, swollen organ plunged to the back of her throat over and over as his hips rolled against her lower jaw the same as they would her lovely little pussy. She left her mouth slack for him, letting him thrust and ride her how he would, green eyes on fire, pleading up at him for more, more.

"This how you'll have it, girl?" Something told him she'd like the lewd words and, with a growl, he fed them to her along with his jutting pride. "On yer knees, choking on a man, servicing a filthy pirate?"

He punctuated the words with enthusiastic pumps and the muffled sounds of her hearty agreement came out around his flesh as glorious, indistinct mewling. Sin rode off his tongue as he provoked her further.

"That's it, lass, take it," he said, easing his movements, spending some time holding himself deep in place at the end of each stroke. His voice was lower now, and he took her hot and slow like molten metal. "Take my cock, Brigit, swallow me up. There's a good girl."

She made some guttural noise at this and he watched her hands claw at her skirts, dragging them up to her hips. Feminine fingers dove between her legs and the maid began to move them over herself in a fury, bucking her hips against the frantic working of her own hand.

The entire picture made his sack draw up tight. The young woman taking her own pleasure, a hand fluttering between her spread thighs. Her jaw parted around his cock, the back of her throat breeched by his every push. And her breasts … she'd never bothered to cover them again during their interruption, and the darkened flesh of her nipples was tight with yearning; the one steady central point on each of her soft, bouncing tits.

It was too much.

"Brigit! Yes! Fuck!"

He buried himself balls deep in the sweet, sweet mouth she offered up, spending the entirety of his pleasure in blinding liquid pulses as her tongue pulled at him, wringing him of every drop.

Her throat closed on him and she took in his release, swallowing down his seed as he twitched and jerked, the spasms of his climax still tossing his body about as a ship on rough waters.

John made to pull himself away as he floated down from his peak, and his eyes opened, ready to give her a chance to breathe but, to his surprise, she clamped her lips firmly around him. The flushed cheeks of the maid hollowed to pull at him still and she made a determined sound, refusing to release his now precariously sensitive member.

A hand still danced between her legs and she leaned towards him now, concentration furrowing her brow as she stroked herself. Desperate noises came from somewhere low in her throat and her head nodded in hurried affirmation. This was what she needed.

He tightened his grip in her hair and planted himself flush to her nose a final time. Brigit fairly screamed around his cock and her humming fingers lost their pace and seized against the crest of her mound with poorly controlled jolts and spasms of movement. Some sound came from her as she crossed the threshold. It might have been laughter or a sob, he couldn't tell.

Either way, after a moment of tense clamping down with her mouth, in which he prayed her teeth would not go any further than they already had, he felt her go limp and she slid away from him in a daze. Brigit slumped to rest her weight on one arm behind her on the floor. Her lowered lashes fluttered dreamily up at him, and he braced his tired body with a palm to the block again, staring back down at her.

"John," she said, eyes serious, "I've never …"

He knew she didn't mean pleasing a man with her mouth. Her talent in that area was stunningly plain. He'd been brought off this way before many a time as well, but still, this had been like none of those.

"I don't think I have either," he said, giving her an exhausted smile.

John pushed away from the block and took a step back, tucking himself back into his breeches. He put a hand out and she took it, climbing to her feet as she adjusted the top of her bodice to conceal her breasts again.

As she righted her clothing and person, he pulled the maid to him again at the waist, taking in the flush of her cheeks and the heightened colour of her lips after what they'd just done.

"Ye make me glad Nassau port is a pirate haven, Mrs O'Creagh," he said to her.

"Why's that?" She seemed properly confused and he gave her a lopsided smile.

"Because even if we go ashore, once ye see the cut of the scoundrels prowling the docks, ye won't want to leave my side for a minute." He ran his thumb over her jaw. "I'll have ye until at *least* the next respectable port."

She turned her face to the side and caught up his thumb,

nipping at it. "I already don't want to leave, Mr Bone."

A surge of feeling welled in his chest and he brushed it away with a jest. "Oh? So there's no reason to truss ye up with a bit of line, just to be sure ye won't run off?"

"Well"—her eyes shone impishly up at him—"at least not today."

Admit defeat now, John Bone. She's got ye wrapped up in a tidy little package.

"Are ye ready for dice tonight?" He made to change the subject, loosening his arms to let her step back if she would.

She didn't.

"Oh yes," she said, those dimples he so liked deepening in her cheeks. "I have to see whether you can look Mr Hawke in the eye or not, now!"

It would be some feat, he allowed, but he'd have to try or she'd be taunting him the rest of the way to Nassau.

As if you'd mind.

It was true, he was growing to like her taunts. He was growing to enjoy a great many things about Brigit O'Creagh.

Here the cook was again, offering her his hand as she stepped up through the hatch just behind him.

Where does a pirate learn manners?

Brigit took hold of the broad, warm fingers and levered herself up the final two steps onto the main deck. Evening meal and the straightening of the galley were behind them, and the promised dicing beckoned. She stood at his side now in the night air, but he didn't release his grasp.

"Now Brigit," he said, leaning in as they made their way along the deck, "these are not *bad* men, truly, but they are a bit rough. I wouldn't be expecting fine language or graceful conversation from this lot, even if their own mothers showed up on the quarterdeck."

She laughed as they strolled in the lantern light towards the raucous sounds of gaming men. "Do you worry about my tender ears, John Bone," she said, tilting her face up to direct the teasing words at him and no one else, "with all your talk just hours ago of me taking your cock?"

The massive bald man at her side sputtered and coughed his way into a deep chuckle at this, and squeezed at her hand anew as they approached the small, but noisy gathering. "Christ, girl," he said as he pulled himself together, "my face'll be as red as my beard. Ye may be worse than half the men."

"Then we shall get on well, Mr Bone." She gave him a final reassuring smile. It was endearing the way he fretted over her meeting the crew outside the routines of meal serving. Brigit had already seen all these men as she filled their cups in the galley, twice a day for the last three days. Though now, she supposed, there was leeway for them to speak more freely with her and Bone, with no plates of food keeping their attention, and no queue for them to hold up with chatter.

The men had circled a number of smallish crates 'round the pool of light at the foot of the main masts for seats, while a larger crate stood as a gaming table in their midst. As Brigit and the cook approached the edge of the circle, the first men to notice them took up cries of welcome, the loudest of which came from the sailor in the garish coat. Mr Grey, if her memory served her.

"Ho there!" he called out, setting his mug down as he stood. "Here's our cook!"

The rest of the eyes turned in their direction then, and Bone volleyed greetings back and forth with a few of them as Grey gestured to a vacant crate which seemed to have been reserved for him.

"Now *here's* the purse you lads want to empty," the little rooster of a man continued as Bone took a seat. "This one almost never joins a game! And if you've seen him part with a coin on shore leave, you've seen one more thing than Simon Grey."

The cook made a rude gesture at the master gunner and both men laughed as Grey sat again to take up his mug and watch the game.

Die made their dull, bouncing clatter atop the central crate, tossed first by the slender Mr Hawke and then by another sailor of about the same age whose name she couldn't remember. The nameless man looked at the pips that landed face up and swore. Hawke clapped his hands together with a bark of laughter at his obvious win and offered to roll again.

Brigit stood at Bone's shoulder now, the only one present still standing. As her eyes made a second, more careful pass around the group, she noticed there was not a single unoccupied crate. Of course the crew hadn't thought of her. She shrugged.

They've already seen you in his bed. He won't mind.

Picking her skirts up to avoid stepping on them, Brigit moved around his bent knee and sat herself squarely atop John Bone's good leg.

"There was nowhere else for me to sit," she said, answering the startled jump of his brows.

"Will there be a proper introduction of the cook's new mate, Mr Bone?" The voice came from the man who'd been losing half his purse to Hawke, now seated and lifting a cup.

The cook shifted and slid an arm around her waist, his hand coming to rest on her hip in a not-so-subtle display of possession. "I'm sure you've all met the widow's maid as you've come through the line for yer last few meals. Captain's sent Mrs O'Creagh to work in the galley for now, considering her lady won't be needing her for a time."

"Did he send her to sit on your knee as well, then?" This from Simon Grey again, to a round of laughter as Bone tugged her closer in his lap.

"Mrs O'Creagh." A few of the men acknowledged the

introduction with her name and a nod before settling back into to their conversations and drinking.

The jocular mood of the crew put Brigit at ease, and she found herself quite comfortable this way, with the side of her body wedged into the crook of Bone's arm. Someone had handed him a drink and he took a long pull, offering it to her as he finished, though she shook her head to decline.

From her perch on his thigh, she cast her eyes around the group, trying to remember names to all these men as she went.

Simon Grey had already made his presence known. It was hard for a body to forget such a loud voice from such a short man. Seated to his right was the cocky William Platt, who smirked at her without a hint of shame, elbows on splayed knees, hands holding a mug, before he went back to half-listening to Grey and watching the next round of dice.

Leaning against the main mast, which stood just afore the boisterous gathering, was Hezekiah, the bosun, as dark a man as Platt was pale, arms folded over his broad chest and grinning from ear to ear at whatever rude jest the gunner was making now.

Henry Adams, the cooper, was speaking with a look of complete seriousness on his face, and great sweeping gestures of his hands to a younger sailor who sat next to the carpenter, Mr George. The rotund, pasty Adams was the one with all the 'pretty words', according to Bone, but Brigit was sceptical.

This is the man who sings?

She'd believe it when she heard it.

The man he spoke to was listening intently, leaning forward with furrowed brows, and Brigit watched as not once, but two or three times, the carpenter's hand moved to light on this man in some discreet way or another. Winters. That was the other man's name. She cocked her head, reading something out of the lack of distance between the two men's crates, the way the carpenter's eye travelled down the deckhand's back.

"John," she murmured into the cook's ear, "Are Mr George and Mr Winters …?

"Aye, Mr George most certainly." His words were quiet and amused, pitched for her alone. "And I suspect Winters as well since the two of them last went ashore."

Brigit let the thought steep for only half a moment before moving on. It would be difficult enough to remember all the names without also having to remember who did what with whom.

"Remind me of the navigator's name again? That's him with the blond hair, isn't it?" She nodded in the direction of the man she meant.

"That'll be Mr Osbourne, and yes, that's him." The cook seemed amenable to her questions and she favoured him with a light kiss to his cheekbone for it.

"And who's that man talking to Mr Hawke now? The one he was throwing dice with?"

"That's Mr Reeve," he answered, "He and Hawke are always up to some bit of trouble or another. You'll see. Those two could have us run aground in the middle of the bloody Atlantic if they were left in command." Bone shook his head and she stifled a giggle at his assessment of the pair. Reeve was as stout as Hawke was lean. Hawke and Reeve, Stout and Lean. That was how she'd remember their names.

Or is it the other way 'round?

The leg she sat on began to bounce a bit as the cook took up tapping his foot in time with some melody which had sprung up from a pipe. She turned her head in the direction of the airy notes to see who was making the music. It appeared the cooper had given up on serious talk, and his one-man audience, Mr Winters, had produced a flute from Heaven knew where. He was now sending up a festive tune, to which Mr Adams was clapping and singing.

Hmm. He is rather good, isn't he?

The man's voice *was* fine, as the cook had told her, but the words to the song, once she paid them more attention, were quite bawdy. A few of the men joined in for the parts of the chorus they knew, chief among them the dirty bits.

Pirates.

Brigit grinned again and kissed John Bone more soundly on the cheek. She was beginning to enjoy herself in this sort of company.

He turned his face to her then and, with a merry glint in his eye, stole a kiss from her lips instead. They were nearly at eye level with each other now, the differences in their height shifted by her sitting on his lap. Her mouth was only just above his, arranged as they were.

Those blue eyes of his caught her up and weren't letting go, and she found her fingertips tracing up along his neck. His free hand came to lace together with the other he'd been holding at her waist, and he pulled her closer, the warmth of his arms a welcome respite from the growing chill of the March evening. Brigit's lips brushed his again and her eyes closed as something fluttered in her belly. They began to kiss as if they weren't surrounded by noisy, gaming sailors.

His jaw tilted into hers and in a moment their tongues were trading places. She felt him then, quite hard against the back of her thigh, and suspected he'd be glad for the concealing drape of her skirts. Her teeth nipped at him and he responded in kind, each vying to steal the other's breath. The whole world swam about them as they enjoyed the taste and hum of the moment.

It came to her between kisses, though, as something out of a fog. The night air of the deck had gone quiet. Adams wasn't singing. Winters had put down his flute. No one was yelling or laughing.

Brigit rolled her face to the side, blinking back into the present with her cheek to the cook's, to find the entire gathering staring at them. Bone's attention came into focus again as well, and he, too, turned his eye back to the men.

An explosion of knowing cries and jeering male laughter went up. Fingers pointed and knees knew the hearty slap of palms. It wasn't every day, it seemed, that the crew of *The Devil's Luck* saw their cook carrying on this way, and they were keen to let him know about it.

"Oi! See here, lads!" crowed Mr Grey, lifting his mug with his voice to be heard over the other men. "Now we know why Mr Bone don't bother to come whoring with the rest of us! He may have a wooden leg and his purse tied shut, but look which one of us has a girl on his knee! Tell us your secrets, John Bone, that we may all be so lucky!"

Brigit blushed at the gunner's words, but she was neither uncomfortable, nor shamed. The arm closest to the cook that she'd draped around his shoulder stayed in place, and for his part he did nothing to release her from the circle of his own arms about her waist.

"The first secret, Mr Grey," he said, grinning across the circle of sailors, "is for a man to learn to use his mouth for more than boasting."

More snorting laughter and salty gibes flew back and forth among the crew at this, and the cook was content to watch them go on as men did once they were warm with drink and trying to best each other with rude remarks.

"At least the cook's mate here looks as though she *wants* to sit on his knee," the navigator put in. "Perhaps Mr Bone should be telling all his 'secrets' to the captain, and give the man an easier time of it."

Platt and Hezekiah had taken up the dice now, but Bone paid little attention.

"What do ye mean, Osbourne?" He leaned a bit to one side to see around the standing pair at their game. The blond man leaned also, elbow on his knee, to elaborate.

"Till sent me to Blackburn's cabin this afternoon to update him on our heading. He had that fine widow right square on his lap, and she looked none too pleased to be there. She wouldn't look in my direction to save her own life."

Brigit tried to picture Mrs Collingwood sitting still on Black Edmund's lap while the navigator had a conversation with the man, and could see the prim widow doing no such thing.

"Did she not stand when you arrived, Mr Osbourne?" Brigit was not timid about joining the conversation herself, and the navigator moved to sit on the crate vacated by Platt, where he'd be closer to her and Bone and not have to shout across the circle.

"Let us say," he replied, fingers smoothing over the angle of his chin, "that your widow and the captain were … otherwise engaged at the time, Mrs O'Creagh. And I don't think he was of a mind to let her up, either." The man tilted his head towards her in implication. Bone grunted.

"Are you telling me you saw them …?" She made a vague gesture with her hands. Brigit was, if not appalled, then surprised at the least. Osbourne shook his head.

"Oh, her skirts had everything properly covered up," he said, "but come now, Missus, a man can tell what he's seeing."

"Are ye so sure, Osbourne?" Bone asked, his voice laced with a note of frustration, more likely over the navigator going further into crude detail in front of Brigit than for any doubt on his part of the veracity of the account. "Maybe ye only thought ye saw." She wasn't nearly as offended as the cook imagined.

"No, Bone, I'm sure," he said, grinning. "And do you know why?"

"Why?" Brigit was the one eager to hear, and she shifted on the cook's lap.

"Because I stood there and gave him my report, and at the end of it I said to him—my exact words, mind you—'Give her one for me, Captain!' " The navigator chuckled at this, but continued. "I only thought to leave after that. I was in there Josephus Rex, of course. Meant to say it as a laugh. But Blackburn says to me—listen to this, Bone—he says"—and here the navigator took pains to imitate the captain's formal tone—" 'I'll give her several Mr Osbourne, if you care to stay and watch.' Can you even imagine such a thing?"

"Hardly sounds like Blackburn at all," Bone muttered. Brigit, however, was knee deep in the delicious scandal.

"And did you?" she pressed him. "Stay and watch?"

The leer all but split the blond man's face in two. "Stood right there by the door until the end of it."

It was beyond imagination. The Widow Collingwood Brigit was accustomed to could teach the word 'prim' itself lessons in modesty. For her to sit there and … and … In front of a stranger, as well?

"And she said nothing, Mr Osbourne? The whole time?" Her curiosity was worse than that furry King George. She saw Bone running his beard through his fingers at all this, in that way she was learning he did when in thought.

"Not a word, Mrs O'Creagh," the navigator said, "but I'll tell you this: the look on her face told a man all he would need to know—though she might've thought she was hiding it. That widow of yours was more than enjoying her welcome aboard *The Devil's Luck*." He tipped down the front of his hat at this with a lecherous wink, confident he'd made his meaning clear.

The cook grunted at this and Brigit was baffled.

Well I'll be damned.

Mrs Hannah Collingwood was up to all sorts of things without a chaperone.

"Do ye think then, Osbourne," Bone returned to the conversation, "the captain will be keeping the widow aboard after Nassau?"

"Oh, I *do* think so, Mr Bone," he said. "Do you know that after I left, I heard he sent for Mr George and had the carpenter bring the widow an entire bucket of *fresh* water?" The blue-grey eyes glittered as he leaned in. "For her to wash up. Sent in *Ellis George*."

A pale arched brow, along with Osbourne's words, seemed to mean more to the cook than it did to Brigit, but whatever the man had just implied caused Bone to relax, at least enough that she felt some of the tension leave the thigh supporting her. She wanted to ask what he meant, but the navigator turned the questions back to the cook.

"What's your worry, Bone? Who cares either way whether he's taken a fancy to this one?"

"If he puts her ashore at the next port," the cook said, "don't ye imagine he'll be sending her maid off, as well?"

Something tiny and brilliant corkscrewed up through her chest.

He's worried you'll be made to leave.

The men exchanged a level glance and then Osbourne was leaning back in realisation. "Ahh, I see," he said, slapping Bone on the shoulder as he took to his feet again. "Well I think you're safe for a while, Mr Bone. Something's afoot with this widow. He even gave her an entire new dress from the slops. Don't tell Grey, though," he said with a chuckle as he moved back to his own crate.

"Don't tell me what?" the gunner chimed in from across the circle.

"Oh, that Bone here's been dunking his balls in the stew for the past two weeks. He didn't want you asking for more than your share!"

Simon Grey shoved the navigator at this, but the sailors were roaring with laughter. "I thought it was a bit saltier, lately!" the gunner fired back, playing along. The cook's shoulders shook with mirth and Brigit leaned in to whisper a private tease at his ear.

"He doesn't know *I'm* the one who's had more than my share, does he, John?"

Bone squeezed her hip at this and rumbled up into the curve of her throat, stopping for a nibble as he went. "Careful, girl, or I'll take ye back down to the galley, right now."

"Will you?" she asked, as though it were a favour rather than a threat.

"Knives!" Osbourne called out, interrupting their saucy

exchange. "Knives! Which one of you lot would like to go a round? Come on!"

There were groans from several of the men, and Brigit turned her attention to see what the navigator was on about.

A sleek throwing knife shone in his hand, and he made a series of flourishes with it, making it glitter over his fingers as he tried to cajole the other sailors into a game. Mr Winter was hauling the central crate that had served for dice out of the circle now, as Osbourne tried for an opponent. The first hint of a smile curled the corner of Brigit's mouth.

"Mr Bone! I've never seen *you* throw! Maybe you've some skill with those hands to make up for that leg of yours?"

"My hands are busy, Osbourne," he lobbed back, taking a familiar squeeze at Brigit's thigh. She gave a warm chuckle at this and nipped at the top of his ear.

"Mr George?" The navigator turned to the carpenter, trying his luck there instead. "You're good with a blade! Three out of four into the mast; that should be an easy wager for you!"

The silver-haired carpenter leaned back on his palms and shook his head with a cool smirk. "Blades are tools, Mr Osbourne, not toys. We have this conversation every time." He had the amused look of a man who had indeed said this same thing on a great many other nights.

"Bah!" Osbourne turned from him, waving him off with a hand, "What about you, Hawke? You almost had me last time!"

The deckhand sighed from where he sat, and Brigit could see none of these men wanted to throw knives with the navigator.

He probably wins every time, and they're tired of handing over coin.

"All right, Osbourne, *one* round," Hawke said, rising resigned from his crate.

"There's a good man! Someone lay out a line!"

Already standing, Winters uncoiled a length of line and drew it out straight, several paces back from the mast, behind which the men were meant to stand and throw.

The rest of the men moved out of the way, although she and the cook were able to remain where they were, as their crate was already the furthest from the path where blades would be flying.

"Would you like to go first, Mr Hawke?" Osbourne extended his hand towards the man. Three additional blades had appeared in it, offered to the deckhand now, handle first.

"No, go on, Osbourne. You go." The tone of his voice told her the younger man had already accepted a likely defeat.

How good could this Osbourne be, really?

"Very well."

The navigator stepped back behind the line and hefted a knife in his hand, the others tucked at the ready into his belt. He held it by the handle, thumb aligned to the blade, she noted. Her eyes narrowed at the placement of his feet, just so.

"Most blades in the mast wins," Osbourne said, glancing at Hawke, "If we land the same number, then we'll see who sticks them in the neatest. Agreed?"

Hawke gave a nod and the navigator went straight to work.

The first knife came back to his ear before following the long arm forward in an arc and spinning out of his grip towards the mast.

Thock.

The tip of the blade bit into the wood, handle angled slightly down. Some noises of approval went up from the other men, and the navigator took up the second knife. Back it went, arc, release.

Thock.

This one landed a foot higher on the mast, and further

to the right, the handle still angled down. Brigit saw what she was dealing with.

The third blade bit, but lower than the other two, the handle straighter this time. Osbourne took a moment longer readying for the fourth and final throw, but this one didn't stick, and clattered to the deck to hooting jeers from the audience.

Hezekiah moved in and picked up the fallen blade before yanking the other three free of the mast and handing them off to Mr Hawke. The lanky sailor moved into position behind the line and Osbourne stepped out of the way.

The deckhand held his shoulders rolled forward in that way some men have who feel awkward being tall. He fumbled a knife into his hand, no stance to speak of, and eyeballed his target. The watching sailors were quiet.

Thock.

His first throw caught, but only just. It was low on the mast and the knife point looked as though it would lose purchase if the wind were to blow. Hawke rolled his eyes and took up a second blade, lobbing it towards the mast with what Brigit would call a sloppy throw. This one spun wide of the mark. Platt and Grey hissed, while she cringed, glad no one else was milling about on the other side of the mast.

Hawke let out a frustrated blast of air through his nose and stood up straighter.

Now he'll try to concentrate.

Thock.

It worked, and the third knife sank in true, centred on the mast. Cheers went up, but Osbourne still smirked from off to the side, fingers laid aside over his lips. Hawke was loose now, with the final knife in his hand.

Ah, but we're too sure after that last one.

A lunge forward and a release, and there went his last blade, bouncing away from the target to meet the same fate as the navigator's fourth throw. He'd made two hits to Osbourne's three.

"Cock and pie!" the deckhand swore, while Osbourne clapped him soundly on the shoulder to the laughter of the rest of the men who knew better from the beginning. Side wagers changed hands and Hawke gave over the coin he'd lost to the victor before flopping back to his seat and taking a long pull from his mug.

"Who's next then?" The navigator brandished the knives in the air again, turning about. "Come on! Hawke can't be the only one with a pair!"

The bridge of her nose crinkled and Brigit popped a knuckle.

"Do you trust me, John Bone?" she said into the cook's ear.

His eyes searched her face in brief confusion before he gave a single nod. "Course I do." There was still a question on his features, but it would do.

"Good."

The maid from Cork rose from the pirate's lap.

"I'll throw against you, Mr Osbourne."

John Bone's eyes tried to pop out of his skull.

"*What?*"

He was not the only one who said it, either. Osbourne and at least a couple more of the crew all blurted the question at once. There was a split second of silence before most of the male portion of the gathering burst into laughter. Sailors thumped crates with palms and the deck with boots, and it was no short time before the navigator could get them all quieted down again.

"*You're* going to throw against *me*, Mrs O'Creagh?"

"I'm fairly certain that's what I said, Mr Osbourne." John looked from the incredulous blond man holding the knives back to Brigit, but she was still and calm, hands at her sides.

"What did you put in her drink, Bone?" Osbourne asked, turning to him. "I think it's gone to her head."

"Don't look at me," John said.

What is she playing at now?

"That is, of course, unless you're afraid to game with someone you've yet to best." The maid was nonchalant, yet John could see something afoot. But what?

"Ohhh! Hear this, you lot!" the navigator called back over his shoulder, rounding again on the gathered crew to gain support for his disbelief. "And have you brought coin to wager, then?"

There. That should settle this. Brigit had already told him her father had snatched up the coin for her service to the widow. She'd come aboard with nothing. He lifted his mug and took in a mouthful of weak ale.

"Mr Bone's purse has yet to be opened," the maid said. "He can meet my share."

John sputtered, choking back the drink so as not to lose most of it down the front of his shirt.

"Picked up a wife in Bristol and you didn't even know it, did you Bone?" Reeve put in from the far side of the group. "Three days in and you're already parting ways with your fortune!"

This brought further convulsions of snickering from all around, but the maid was still the eye of the storm.

"Three out of four into the mast," she said to Osbourne, "same as Mr Hawke, and double his purse if I do." The man was agog, and then folded in half with great peals of laughter.

"Double his purse!"

Double? Is she mad?

"Hellfire, I'll give double *my* purse if she lands *one*," Platt grumbled from his seat as he swished his drink around in its cup.

Thank God he'd brought only a token purse above decks tonight, and left the bulk of his coin locked up in the galley. He sighed and shook the leather bag in the air, clinking the coins together for his answer.

"Do we have a wager, Mr Osbourne?" she asked.

The navigator assessed the maid with a cunning smile and a downward tip of his chin. "All right, Mrs O'Creagh. We do." He handed the knives to her like Old Nick making a deal and flashed a set of teeth in her direction. "I'll even let you throw against my earlier set, so I've no chance for the full four."

"That's very kind of you," she said, reaching for the blades. John saw her grip fumble, and two of the knives spilled from her grasp to the deck with a dull thud. She hopped back with a curse to get her feet out of the way of the falling steel points. The navigator bubbled with laughter.

"Would you like a practice throw or two, Mrs O'Creagh?" he asked her, knowing indulgence dripping from his words. "Courtesy for a lady, of course."

The crew conveyed their loud amusement at this as Brigit bent to retrieve the two dropped knives. She turned her face back to him then and, hidden by her skirts and meant only for him to see, her fingers took up one of the blades with a nimble flourish. Amid the cackling and howling of the crew she gave him wink that all but curled his whiskers before standing again with the four knives in hand.

Do you trust me, John Bone?

He grunted to himself.

What's her game?

"I imagine that's wise," she said to Osbourne, accepting his offer. "Two for practice then?"

The navigator nodded with a smile and stepped out of her way, and she moved to stand behind the line.

A knife was in her hand and she brought it back over her shoulder, a look of fierce concentration on her face.

Brigit stepped forward and the blade flew.

It wobbled across the distance in a clumsy arc and glanced from the right side of the mast, hitting the deck on its flat side and spinning a few feet farther away. John's instinct told him to bury his face in his hands, but that scorching wink she'd sent his way made him keep his eyes open in morbid curiosity.

Brigit shook her head and made a noise of displeasure, taking up another blade for her second throw.

This one sailed with more force, but still with a similar lack of form.

Thock.

It bit into the wood, though, if just barely, and low. Perhaps at waist height. She screwed up her face at the result and walked the gauntlet of smirking men to retrieve the steel from the target herself, slipping past to gather up the blade that had flown wide, as well.

Furious wagering was going on now all around them as the maid returned to the line, hands fidgeting with the bundle of knife handles once she stood there. John was fussing as well, with the tin rose and bull charms at the ends of his braids.

Come on, girl. These men will eat ye alive.

"Shall we let her stand on the near side of the line, lads, so she'll have a fighting chance?" Osbourne was playing to the crowd, ever the gamesman.

The maid already stood behind the line, as the men had, but she narrowed her eyes now at the man needling her and took a step backwards.

"Oohh!" More cries went up from the men. She stepped back again.

And again.

A low whistle went up and now hushed voices rippled around the circle. John was still and tense in his seat, arms folded over his chest.

"She can't be serious," Winters said, leaning in for a hoarse aside to the carpenter. Ellis George shrugged and shook his head.

This had better be worth it, pretty girl.

Every eye was on the cook's new mate as she tucked three of the knives halfway into the waistband of her apron, while keeping one in hand. The navigator stood off to the side, opposite John, with a smug grin.

"Are you ready, Mrs O'Creagh?"

"As I'll ever be," she said, fingering the point of the blade in a considering manner.

John realised he was holding his breath.

Beneath layers of skirts and petticoats, it was harder to judge her stance, but as her hand came back to her ear he saw she held the knife by the blade instead of the handle, unlike her opponent.

Is … is she …?

The plump curves of the body he'd been crushing and squeezing with greed these last three days moved forward in a sleek momentum now, and it was at that moment John Bone knew the navigator was well and properly buggered.

It was quick and graceful, the merciful taking of a life in battle. Her movements came in the same pattern as Osbourne's had, only more fluid, more precise. A song of flying steel to the braying of an ass.

The first knife no sooner left her fingers than the second was flashing in her hand, following the same, clearly practised arc.

Thock. Thock.

Holy Hell!

She had the third one palmed before he even had time to tear his eyes away from the first pair planted stiffly in the mast. The final blade glittered past her cheek and was gone, following the straight path of her outstretched arm upon release.

THOCK!

A man could have heard a rat sneeze.

There they were: one, two, three. The knives made a neat line down the mast, one beneath the other, several inches apart each, and handles straight out, as though she'd walked up and jammed them into the wood on a mark.

"I believe I needed only three of the four, Mr Osbourne?" Her tone was casual, but the barest hint of satisfaction was rolling in at the edges. The navigator had stuck three in the mast as well, but his had been at all angles and here and about, not in an impossibly clean row.

A riot nearly erupted on the deck. Howls of disbelief from sailors who'd lost coin, and barking, wailing laughter from those who hadn't. The navigator could do no more than stand there with his mouth open, staring at the tidy array of blades. The row from the group was enough that John was surprised the quartermaster didn't come storming out to lay into them about it.

His face was in pain, and he realised it was from the size of his grin. She looked back at him over her shoulder and gave a cheeky toss of her head to go with the mischievous smirk on her lovely mouth.

"Where's the fourth one?" Hawke piped up over the din.

It was true, no one had seen her throw the last blade.

"That's probably the one she missed," said the cranky Platt, who'd just bet and lost his purse twice.

John saw the gleam of metal plucked from her apron when it was already too late.

Thock!

The final blade flew and stuck, pinning the end of the red sash Platt wore at his waist to the front of the crate where he sat, inches from his pride, jutting from the wood in a plain statement.

"I don't miss, Mr Platt."

The cook swelled with pride.

At this there was more hooting from the men, and some of them even stepped in to thump Brigit on the shoulder as though she were one of the crew. He levered himself up from his seat and got his stiff leg under him to move in her direction, not sure if he approved of other men touching her, even in this way.

Platt glowered down at the knife once he'd started his heart beating again, and yanked it out of the wood with a snort of disgust. He handed it off to the still dumbfounded Osbourne and shook his head, standing and stretching. John could tell he was ready to find his hammock.

"Christ, man!" Simon Grey put in, gesturing at Brigit, "Don't let this one near the flats and sharps when she's in a mood!"

John arrived behind her and she felt his presence, stepping back to put her back at his chest and let his arms come around her.

"You'll want to collect from Mr Osbourne, John," she said turning her face up and tugging him down by the braids of his beard for a bold kiss.

At that moment, he wanted to collect from *her*.

Brigit O'Creagh felt right in his arms. She had a filthy mouth. And apparently she was dangerous.

I think I'm in love.

"Where the devil did ye learn to throw like that?" he asked, chuckling as they broke apart from their kiss.

"My da's friends," she said into the side of his neck, "Mum would send me to fetch him, but he'd be full as a goat half the time when I got to the pub, and passed out, and I'd game with his mates until he woke up. Or I'd win enough coin to pay one of them to help me cart him home."

"Ye certainly 'had a game' with Osbourne, pretty girl," he said, moving his hands lower to squeeze her at the hips. Men were milling about now; the gathering had that tentative feeling where people suggested the hour and stifled yawns.

She wriggled her backside against him and gave a satisfied little *humph*. "That man pisses more than he drinks," she said, "It's easy to boast when you're not accustomed to losing."

The man in question was approaching them now, and Brigit untangled herself from his arms to step to the side.

"Here, you old sea-crab." The navigator dangled a purse at him from between two fingers, wearing a lopsided smile. "I should have known you were up to something."

"I wasn't up to *any*thing, Osbourne," he said, as he took the full purse and transferred its coin to his own, handing back the empty bag. "If I knew she could handle a knife like that, ye think I would have handed her one on her first hour in my kitchen and told her to peel potatoes?"

"Or tried to stand there and steal kisses all the while?" she asked, poking him in the ribs.

"Hah!" the blond man barked, pocketing the purse, "Well I shall know to think twice when you're eager to wager in the future, Mrs O'Creagh. I'm sure Mr Bone will be on his toes, as well."

"Aye, all five of them," John said, thumping his peg on the deck.

Osbourne wandered away shaking his head and John took the opportunity to press the small bag of coin into Brigit's palm.

"Ye earned it, pretty girl," he said still wearing a disbelieving smile.

"No need for all that, Mr Bone," she said, folding the prize back into his grip. "What would I spend it on, any way? I only made the bet to see the look on Mr Osbourne's face." Her soft smile turned mischievous now. "And maybe yours, a bit."

"But ye could go anywhere," he said, his conscience making him speak out against his selfish desires, "once we make port. Buy passage back home. Or to the colonies, if ye like."

She'd stepped close during his half-hearted suggestions and those green eyes looking up were yanking at things in his chest.

"I don't know that I *want* to go anywhere else, Mr Bone." Her voice was low, lips slightly parted. He swallowed.

Had there been a point in his life where he'd stopped to decide whether he had a firm opinion on the existence of witchcraft?

The spell was broken, however, by the gunner, who had climbed up to stand on one of the crates, mug in hand.

"Let's raise our drinks, men, before we head below for the night!"

There were nods and calls of approval, and men took up cups all around. Brigit slipped behind him and retrieved his own mug from beside the crate where he'd left it, handing it back to him in time for the toasts.

That was kind; to save me the walk back.

He pulled her to his side again with an arm at her waist, loathe to stand there and not touch her. She slid her fingers over the top of his, a silent approval of his gesture.

"First," Grey began from atop the crate, "to Edmund Blackburn! The captain chooses our battles well and keeps our purses full! A man could never want to sail on a finer ship than *The Devil's Luck*!"

"To the captain!" Drinks rose, tilted back.

"And then, to Benjamin Till! Other quartermasters might forbid gaming on their ships, but not ours! And for that we've had a fine time of it tonight!"

"To Mr Till!" They drank again, and he planted a noisy smack with his lips at Brigit's temple, though she seemed content to watch without drinking herself.

"To Hezekiah!" the gunner said, gesturing at the bosun with his mug, "Without sails and line we'd get bloody nowhere, and since that's where we've all come from, I'm sure none of you louts are interested in going back!"

More laughter and drinking. "To Hezekiah!"

"To William Osbourne! He's taken the bother to learn numbers and the use of a back staff, so the rest of us will never have to. *And* he pulls a fantastic face when a young woman bests him at knives!"

The crew roared at this, and the navigator shook his head. "To Mr Osbourne!"

"To Henry Adams! May the cooper keep all the barrels water-tight, lest they drain and we all have to take our turns inside!"

John nearly lost his drink at that one. He glanced at the maid, but she seemed unaware. The cooper's considerable gut wobbled with coughing laughter, and Winters had to slap him on the back.

"To Mr Adams!

Grey gestured at the carpenter, next. "To Ellis George, who keeps our fine ship in fine shape. Never did I know a man who could so well work the wood."

"To Mr George!"

The carpenter smirked and made a rude gesture at Mr Grey, and Winters turned a conspicuous shade of red.

"To Simon Grey!" the gunner said, and winked down at Brigit, "That's me, lass." She shook her head, and gave the man a roll of her eyes. "The ships don't raise a white flag, but they've had the count of our guns. And you should all be honoured to sail aboard the ship what sports the longest gun on the Atlantic, my friends!" The gunner made a lewd grab at the front of his breeches to groans and jeers from half the men, though they laughed any way.

"Christ, Grey," John muttered as he repeated the gunner's name, raising his mug with the rest, but not drinking as it was now emptied. The maid only giggled.

"To John Bone!" he called out. Brigit looked up at him, smiling. "Without this great, bald bastard, we'd all starve before we made it to Nassau!"

"To Mr Bone!" The toast was hearty and eyes were on him. The maid nudged at him with her hip.

"And last," Grey said, "to Brigit O'Creagh! Without her, *the cook* would starve before we made it to Nassau, and we can't have that!"

The men lost their minds at this, and to John's surprise, Brigit was laughing as well. He felt her arm move 'round his waist and then she had a handful of his backside.

"To Mrs O'Creagh!"

The sailors drank but, as John's mug was drained, he turned to the young woman in his arms. The woman who swore, who threw knives, who fetched his drink to save him pain. Those green eyes were full of warmth, and the smile, the dimples … The cook was unmanned. He kissed her. Thoroughly.

We've sailed off the edge of the map now, John Bone. We have, indeed.

Brigit woke with a sudden intake of breath, her heart in her chest, right hand gripping the edge of the narrow berth where she laid on her side. Her cheeks were hot, as though she'd been crying, but there were no tears.

She let the air take its slow leave of her lungs as her growing familiarity with the surrounding hold came settling in around her like an embrace. It must have been some time in the wee hours of morning. The oil lamp burned on the wall near the stair, as it should. Sailors snored in their gently rocking hammocks, as they should. And a heavy, comforting arm lay draped across her waist.

As it should.

Wide awake now, and blinking into the dim light, Brigit furrowed her brow at the sense of … awfulness that had wrenched her out of her dream. Something foul, sullied, which could never be washed clean. The memories of any part of it that made sense were already dissipating beyond her ability to grasp at them and form anything coherent.

There had been cannon fire, wood splintering. She'd stood at the gunwale of a ship, wearing breeches like a man, saying something weary to a young woman she'd never met. And then there had been a man. It was *this* image that had rattled her awake.

Brigit didn't know his face, but yet she did. His mouth had been wide in some silent scream, and a blade was buried deep in his right eye socket. Another was lodged in his moving throat, and a third stuck out from his chest. There was blood, and a great lot of it. And, in her dream, Brigit knew she had put those blades there herself.

Take a deep breath, you're awake now girl.

She calmed herself again, and sniffled, louder than she might have liked. There had been knife throwing tonight, and her carrying on with a group of men, so why shouldn't she dream of such things? The true rub was that now she was wide awake, and unlikely to fall asleep again any time soon.

She shifted her hips and pointed her feet straight down in a carefully controlled stretch, trying to relax again and invite drowsiness.

A male thigh moved against the back of her leg, and the cook's forearm tightened around her. He stirred, making some low, nearly inaudible noise with his face in her hair, and she burrowed her body back into his, enjoying the movements and sounds of the man in his sleep.

But there were lips on her shoulder now, and the arm 'round her middle didn't ease up in its hold. Fingers splayed across her belly.

"Mmm … Brigit …"

Oh, for the love of—! Now you've gone and woken him up, too!

And not just him. There was a hum, a tingle she'd grown accustomed to, that flared to life now. One that always seemed to appear whenever John Bone touched her. One that started just between her thighs.

Well. Perhaps if we are *both awake …*

She tilted her shoulders to better face him. There he was, so, so close. Those eyes that saw her as something worthwhile. That soft, wicked mouth.

A small movement of her jaw angled her face up towards his, and their lips came just into contact. Their eyes traded a silent song, a nameless joyful suffering, and time seemed to stretch out. Her chest was rising and falling with breaths that came shorter, and her eyes were burning hot under threat of an outburst of new emotion.

The arm at her waist slid over her side and around her shoulder, and now she felt the barest touch of a fingertip just beneath her chin. Brigit roiled with tension.

Oh God! Oh God, this man!

The pad of his finger began to trace a delicate, excruciating path down the front of her throat. It seemed to go on for days, and she was driven near to madness by this silken, feather of a caress coming from the same man who'd called himself 'large and clumsy' that very morning.

Brigit was nearly squirming by the time the fingertip reached the hollow of her throat, the cupid's bow of her upper lip still no more than brushing his. She swallowed. Neither had closed their eyes or torn their gaze away from the other. Now his forefinger was sliding off to the side of her neck, his thumb opposite, so the column of her throat was under his palm. The tips of his fingers curled ever so gently into the meat between her neck and shoulder. While almost completely still, they rushed towards something. Something …

"John," she whispered against his mouth, "I—"

The kiss happened then, scattering thought aside.

Everything was so warm, so perfect. Lips a sweet prayer and that tongue such a scorching blasphemy. Oh, how she'd needed this man. It only took her being led astray onto a pirate ship to find him.

The hand at her throat grew restless and slipped back down to her hip where fingers, gentle moments ago, pulled her back against the massive frame of his body with a rough urgency. There he was, hard as stone, pressed to her backside in a wordless confession of need. He crowded her at the outer edge of the bunk with a slow churn of his hips, and Brigit pushed herself back, shameless, surrounding his erection with her body's curves as he ground himself into them.

As they kissed, and though it was awkward, she managed to snake a hand behind her and was able to fumble and root her way into his breeches. When she found him he was scalding hot to the touch, and she filled her grip with his swollen shaft, way down at the base.

He hissed, as if he'd been burnt, trying to keep his voice low. "Brigit!"

Mmm, there *he is. There's my man.*

A small door opened somewhere in Brigit's mind then, as she accepted the weight of this thought. She was, indeed, beginning to think of John Bone as her own.

She gave him a healthy squeeze and he pulsed in her hand. Her thighs slid together, wet from arousal. Brigit needed him, now.

No one else is awake. We can be quiet …

"Please, John," she breathed between kisses, "love me."

There was little time for her to contemplate her choice of words.

Her grip on him tightened around more than merely his aching prick.

What did she just say?

John drew back from a string of kisses that had blurred his world like strong drink to see her eyes, dark and pleading in the lamp light. Something compressed under his ribs.

He glanced around the hold. It was either very early or very late, but still, they were the only two awake.

Hell, a man only has so much will power.

Especially when the maid looked at him that way, on fire with want.

He descended on her then, nudging her hand out from between them, grabbing up fistfuls of skirts and petticoats, piling up fabric at the small of her back. Even if a sailor or two were awake, he had no faith he could stop now.

Breeches shoved clear of his raging lust, John angled himself and slid with agonising relief into the hollow between thighs and bare pussy. She tightened her legs around him in response and he ploughed through the lush furrow, stifling a groan at the soaking mess he found waiting there.

John watched her chew at her lower lip, eyes closed, holding back whimpers of her own. He wished he could have her elsewhere. In a proper bed, away from a sleeping crew. They could make noise, they could scream and beg for each other. He wanted that. Wanted to hear her cry out, call his name, make demands for him not to stop with that salty mouth of hers.

And mayhap one day you will, John. But for now, shut up and give the woman what she wants.

He tilted his hips to a shallower angle, bringing himself to press at her entrance. She looked back at him again, expectant.

"Brigit," he whispered, "do ye want me?"

Those eyes were unblinking and swallowed him whole.

"I want you John, *please*."

He surged forward. One moment he was without, the next within. She was so unbelievably wet the barest movement of his hips saw his cock sheathed to the root. And with her thighs clenched together this way she fit tight around him, even more than she had their first time. It was enough to make his teeth grind together.

Keep a hold of yourself, man.

But he wanted to fuck. To have her. John began to push, to take. He would show her what she did to him, but it was madness. She was too hot, too close around him, and her mouth was open in a wordless picture of pleasure, eyes nearly black with need, saying *Give me! Give, give.*

His fingers dug into her hip and he held himself still. How was a man expected to hold up this way? He'd be done in moments if it went on like this.

Think of her then, instead, you great ox.

The smile welled up from his insides before curling up on his lips. Yes, he should think of her.

The hand at her hip burrowed its way beneath fabric now, tracing a path back over the same territory, only free of obstacles. His fingers slid along the cleft where her thigh met her body, and beyond that the curls between her legs. He dipped between slick folds, searching.

The tiny chirp of delight she wasn't able to supress told him he'd found what he wanted. He began to stroke and circle his fingertips, holding his cock firmly in place within her core, trying to keep his own pleasure to a minimum, lest he end things before they began. Like all women, however, she couldn't help but make things difficult.

Brigit would not hold still. He'd halted his thrusts, but she wouldn't have it and arched into him, writhing on his cock, squirming, stroking him with the grasping walls of her pussy as his fingers fluttered between her lips. Fuck. This was not helping.

No! Not yet, John!

Her head whipped back to him, eyes wide and desperate, and her wrist twisted to grab at the braids of his beard. With a sharp tug, she brought him down for a frenzied kiss and her lovely round hips humped at him in a fury. He could almost hear the apology in her tone as she gave up her muted, urgent sounds into this mouth. His hand worked between her legs, tenacious, determined.

Come for me, girl. For the love of God! Before I—

She went stock still, eyes wide. Feminine flesh clutched around him. Her body pulled at his prick, rippling, sucking at him; excruciating.

John held his ground, gritting his teeth as her shuddering worked its way to an end. The look on that face of hers as she floated down nearly had him undone.

She was his. He knew. Her eyes told him.

He needed to be still.

John took a deep, slow breath, and brought his tired hand over her hip and lightly raked his nails up the back of her thigh, enjoying the feel of the muscle there tightening in response. His caress was stopped along the way by a ripe handful of bottom, and he took time to knead at the plump cheek. She sighed and rolled into his touch, and the feel of her, cushioned up against him that way, impaled on his cock, brought him into a new surge of lust.

His thumb pressed into the soft globe of flesh, and it slid, suggesting, along the cleft of her bottom, even before his mind had the words. John was filled with unreasonable desires. The pad of his thumb brushed over that hidden pucker and Brigit inhaled sharply.

Behave yourself, John.

But he wanted to do no such thing. She made his mind spin with depravity. The things he would do with her, if she'd allow. He swirled the thumb about, lazy, exploring. If Brigit O'Creagh was his, he wanted to claim her in every way possible. And there was one way, right in front of him now, he hadn't.

In the same way a body drifts, well on its way to sleep, and then is jarred awake by a sudden sense of falling, Brigit was sobered out of her hazy reeling by the feeling of John Bone's thumb tracing a path where no thumb had any occasion to be.

Had she not been limp as a rag from her own release, moments ago, she might have gasped, or stiffened. The contented fog she floated in now, however, stripped her of tension and left her merely curious. She turned her face back to him, wrinkling the bridge of her nose and cocking her head in unspoken question.

The cook arched a mischievous brow at her and circled his thumb with more pressure, massaging at the knot of flesh while his cock remained buried inside her. That he'd yet to reach his own climax was a fact not lost on Brigit. She was sobering up now, and fast.

He'd nudged at this same forbidden opening once before, that first night as he'd pleasured her with his mouth. Just a tickle from his little finger then, enough added sensation to help send her over the edge. Now it was more than a nudge.

The cook held her gaze, watching her for denials as the thumb dipped. Her heart beat faster, and she opened her mouth, but only to breathe and hold fast to blue eyes. If he went on this way, there would come a point where …

Her breath hitched. The tip of his thumb was in, circling, and then pressing deeper. She felt the glow of warmth between her legs kindle to life again at this new, strange stimulation, and Bone added to it with a slow, deliberate movement of his hips, withdrawing and sheathing himself again. It was too much, this, and she wanted to cry out, and irrationally, to slap him for doing these things to her while she had to remain silent.

The timbers of the hull creaked passively with the subtle rise and fall of the ship, and around them men made quiet sounds in their sleep. If the frustrated groans and whimpers she held narrowly in check were to erupt now, she'd wake the whole crew.

Damn you, John Bone, what will you have? Stop torturing me!

His languorous pumping ceased, but now he stroked at her from inside with the impertinent thumb. The cook lowered his lips to her ear and spoke, barely audible.

"Brigit … have ye had a man this way before?"

Her body clutched at him in shock and unexpected arousal, which brought another reminder that both her entrances were still full of pirate.

He's not making conversation, Brigit. He wants permission.

Could she give it?

She knew this was done, and knew she might expect it to hurt. A stray thumb was one thing; an entire stiff prick was another. Though the subtle way he was easing it in and out now, while he awaited her response, was not altogether unpleasant. And the idea of him having her in this forbidden way, taking what no other man had yet taken …

Yes. She wanted to give this to him. Let him take pleasure from her body any way he wanted it. The thoughts alone were overwhelming.

"No, John," she whispered, answering his question, "I haven't."

His eyes were on her, expectant. She gave him what he wanted.

"Be my first."

He thrust into her then, her words making his hips buck on their own, a pained look on his face as he bit his lip. It seemed her assent itself drove him closer to the edge.

The thumb left her, and only an odd sense of vacancy remained. His kisses fell at her shoulder, her throat, before catching up her mouth again as he plunged home into her pussy several more times for good measure. Just as she began to press back into this rhythm, however, he withdrew to accept her offer. Now the hard length of him was gliding, slick, over the newly awakened ring of flesh between her cheeks.

She heard the blood pulsing at her temples, a surging rush to echo her thoughts.

Oh God, oh God, Brigit, he's going to. He's really going to.

The first nudge lit her up. Her eyes were wide as she felt the blunt steel of him begin to circle, to press. He spread her own moisture around with the warm, fleshy head of his cock, intent, she judged, on easing his passage. When the pushing began in earnest, however, she went entirely still.

It was a curious feeling. When she held it in her hand or her mouth, the end of his shaft was plump, supple. Now that he made to enter her this way, it felt condensed to a hard, narrow point, bent on spearing into her. Brigit felt herself begin to open to him.

Heaven help me, this is it!

John brushed a kiss over her ear. "Calm down, pretty girl," he whispered. "Let me in. Let me have ye."

It was his voice that did it. Brigit let go.

The stretch as the tight band of muscle accepted the first rigid male inch was like nothing she'd known. There was a hint of a burn as her confused little rosebud adjusted to the new intrusion their efforts asked it to accommodate, but then a delicious ... *wrongness* ... as this normally ignored part of her body received the lusty attentions of a man.

His hand moved back to her hip now, no longer needed to angle himself into place, and he began the tortuous process of working his remaining length up into her bottom.

Brigit lay there on her side, somehow wonderfully helpless in the ship's hold, as the cook took up a slow pattern of press and withdrawal, rooting his impossibly firm girth further inside as he went. The swollen folds of her sex were throbbing with abandon now, vacant, envious of the male flesh filling her backside.

And there he was. She felt the soft press of his balls up against her, and knew he'd seated himself to the hilt. The hand at her hip came to splay across her belly and their eyes locked, blue on green.

The look on her face must have been pleading now, as she held his gaze over her shoulder. His brow furrowed with concern and she saw he was worried about pressing on, about hurting her with movement now that he'd filled her. But what she begged for with her eyes was not for him to hold back.

"Go on, John," she breathed, "let me feel you."

Brigit felt him. Oh, did she feel him. The withdrawal was almost total, and her nerves went wild with new sensation, but the next full, smooth plunge stuffed her again to the brim, intense and utterly foreign. Her mouth came open in a silent curse. How many strokes like these could she take, Brigit wondered, before she went mad?

Her neck relaxed as she surrendered to the experience, and as her head lolled forward again she found herself staring blankly into the hold. Bone was working her now, his movements slow and careful, and her inner thighs slipped with wetness at the thrill of being taken.

She became aware, however, through her carnal haze, that she and the cook were no longer the only two stirring in the crowded cabin.

In the hammock straight across the walkway, a man was awake. Staring at them. Brigit's breath stopped. It was Hawke. And he had his cock in a lazy hand, stroking.

She froze, clenched. Movement behind her stopped, and she tilted her face back to hiss at Bone, while keeping her eye on the deckhand.

"John," she said, low and urgent, "Mr Hawke is awake. He's watching us."

Of all things, she felt a shadow of a chuckle rumble through his chest at this, and he kissed at her jawline.

"Did ye want to stop now, love?" he asked her, voice low but playful. "Or shall we give him a bit of a show?"

Brigit gaped at him.

"He'll have naught but the palm of his hand until at least Nassau, the poor bastard." Bone smirked at this, but then his features grew serious. "But we'll stop, if ye want."

She didn't want to stop, but … With an audience? Could she?

The whole crew already knows you sleep in his bed, girl. They've guessed what you're up to, whether they've seen it or no.

He throbbed inside her, making her tingle and stretch as he waited for her word. Right. She wanted John Bone more than she wanted the deckhand to go back to sleep. Brigit arched back into her lover, pushing herself down onto his erection for her response.

With a barely audible growl, he accepted, bent on having her now, prying eyes be damned. Her encouragement seemed to have cut some restraining band of caution loose and the cook pushed deep, letting small grunts of effort escape as he delivered his lust up into her. Thick manhood sank in again and again, raw, searing, decadent.

It was all Brigit could do not to cry out, while he split

her in two this way, and Hawke's keen eye in their direction made it quite difficult for her to focus on remaining silent. Her first instinct was to shut her eyes and block out the deckhand's intent stare, but a moment or two of the crude attempt at blinders proved it a failure. She could all but feel his gaze on them. Her eyes came open again and, sure enough, there was Hawke, staring, tugging at himself with a purpose.

Bone's hand at her hip wandered up, groping at her breast, squeezing, pulling her roughly to him. She ground back to receive his thrusts now, a slow warmth creeping over her belly as she discovered something peculiar about being watched.

It excited her.

The deckhand's eyes raking over their coupled, writhing form, his hand stroking, intent, as the cook had his way … She was catching fire, piece by piece. A squeak of overwhelmed passion slipped out when she tipped her head back against the wall of Bone's chest.

"Shh, now," he warned. At least one of them had enough sense to remember they needed quiet. The male arm she'd been trapping under her neck curled in now, and he laid his first two fingers over her lips in reminder.

Lovely idea, John.

Brigit opened her mouth and drew him in, sucking at the fingertips, pulling him deeper with her swirling tongue. She felt his teeth at her shoulder, biting in to stifle his own groans at this blatant imitation of her gift to him in the galley earlier that day.

Her pussy hummed with envy, as empty as her backside was full, and the rate of his pumping increased. He pulled his fingers from her mouth and caught up her right hand, guiding it down over her stays, and then lower.

"I'm close, pretty girl," he rasped at her ear. "Touch yourself. Come with me."

The request stunned her, flooded her hungry sex with a wanton heat.

Yes.

Her hand burrowed, urgent, finding its way clear beneath her skirts. Bone plunged from behind, unrepentant for his harsh strokes.

Yes, yes, oh YES.

Her fingers hit their mark. She found herself beyond soaked, and went straight to work, giving Hawke more of a show now than she'd ever intended.

She didn't care.

Delicate folds and a sensitive little pearl shimmered with flashes of pleasure under the frenzied movements of her own hand, and the cook was solid, driving, relentless behind her.

Their sinful dance reached a thrumming, fever pitch, and Bone bore down, nearly rolling her onto her stomach with the zeal of his efforts. The added weight against her back and the insistent pumping crushed her busy fingertips right up against her most sensitive flesh, and Brigit seized up, still and tight.

Her climax crashed into her, an explosion of light and excruciating joy that spun away from her centre in glittering shards of paradise.

Oh God! Yes! God, John, yes! I love you!

Her body clutched at him, walls fluttering as she came. Muscles inside her rippled over his cock, demanding surrender, insisting he join her in bliss.

As she spasmed and jerked her way through her release, Brigit felt him go impossibly hard. He drove into her in a last, feral thrust, his whole body becoming rigid, growling through his teeth before he could stop himself.

She felt the first pulses, and then the wicked jet of hot seed inside her as he tripped over the edge. He held himself there, thumping exquisitely into her bottom, the warm fluid of his spending now letting her slide on his prick in smooth luxury. Brigit wallowed in the feeling, rolling her hips, hoping to milk him for all he had to give. She wanted all of it, all of him.

His breath was heavy now as he came down, fingers of his free hand cupping over her shoulder. Her head tilted back for a kiss and they lapped each other up, a glowing thanks for shared ecstasy.

The cook was still buried as deep as he might go and working to take slower, calmer breaths. Her fingers relaxed and moved from between her legs, grabbing a handful of skirts as she went and pulling them down to cover herself again. His lips were gentle now, moving to her jaw. A hand found hers and he laced their fingers together, bringing his mouth to her knuckles, as well.

Brigit's head rolled to the side under the sweetness of his touch and found their audience at an end. Hawke's back was to them now, and he appeared to be dead asleep. It was anyone's guess whether he'd found his own release, but that mattered little just now.

At the peak of her pleasure the words had come ringing out in her mind.

I love you.

Did she? Was Brigit O'Creagh in love with this pirate? And if she was, did she dare tell him?

The thoughts beat at her like gusts of wind, even as the man at her back softened and slid from her body, unaware. There were kisses at her shoulder now, but they were drowsy. The cook was dragging her petticoats back into place, pulling her close, ready to drift into sleep.

Had she loved anyone before now? She didn't think so. No man had made her come apart this way. Be this reckless, brazen. She was more at home now, it seemed, than she'd ever been in the tiny house overflowing with parents and siblings.

Bone gave her a faint squeeze, and murmured into the back of her neck, fading fast.

"See ye 'n the morn, pretty girl."

The words felt easy and right, and she relaxed into his embrace. Perhaps this *was* what it felt like.

Her thoughts disintegrated, tumbling her towards sleep.

The Devil's Luck. And maybe now Brigit's luck, as well.
I'm in love with a pirate.

John thumped his way back to the galley from the lower gun deck. Simon Grey had decided that since the cook was in charge of meals, he was therefore also in charge of the mess, and that included the supervision of wrangling a stuck table down from its chains in the ceiling. This apparently required four men and a bucketful of swearing.

But then again, anything done properly on a ship required swearing.

He moved across the main deck beneath a sun well past the top of its arc for the day, eager to return to the maid. There were matters on his mind, and he wanted her ear.

Just see it past Nassau, John. Don't be hasty.

"Mr Bone!"

"Captain," he said, turning back to the approaching man. Blackburn's fine coat flapped in the breeze, and John noted some ease to the serious look the man spent most of his time wearing.

"Have you given your list of supplies to Mr Till yet, Bone?" Blackburn always moved straight to business.

"Aye, Captain. Did that this morning." He crossed his arms over his chest and shifted his weight off his peg.

"And your new mate? Suitable? I've heard rumours already, Bone." The captain cracked a smile at this, a rare event. "Knives? And Osbourne lost a purse?"

John chuckled at the memory of the navigator's open mouth at the sight of the three blades. "Ye should have seen it, Captain. We could have dropped an anchor down his gullet. Aye, she's quite suitable, Sir. And I'm glad for the extra pair of hands."

"I'm sure you are, Mr Bone," Blackburn smirked at him, "I'm sure you are. You'll be wanting her aboard beyond

Nassau, then?"

Ah, here was the very matter he'd been afraid to address. "I do indeed, Captain, if it can be permitted."

"And does she wish to remain?"

"I suspect she might, Sir." He had high hopes after the previous night.

"Then we'll draw her a contract like everyone else," he said, "But Bone—you'll see there's no trouble made with the other men. Women aboard? Well … we need to keep order, you understand."

"Of course, Captain." Blackburn hadn't heard rumour then, it seemed, that John had made it clear he'd tolerate no foolishness from the crew in that regard.

"Very well, Bone."

"And how fares the widow, Captain?" John couldn't help his curiosity, especially after that wild story from Osbourne. Blackburn's brows raised in surprise at this question, but he answered all the same, unusually forthcoming.

"The widow is … not 'accustomed' to men such as ourselves, Bone. I'm attempting to remedy this fact. Till tells me she's quite amenable, but that remains to be seen." A new mischief glinted in the captain's eye, and John both wanted to know and didn't.

"Women!" was all he could say, taking the risk of clapping the dark-haired man on the shoulder with gruff familiarity.

"Indeed, Bone." Blackburn nodded, eyes focusing elsewhere. "Well? Carry on."

"Aye, Sir."

John turned back in the direction of the galley, heartened by the captain's approval of the maid.

As though summoned by the lift of his mood, he saw the top of her head surface through the hatch. Brigit mounted the stair to the deck as he approached, smiling when she caught sight of him, cheeks dimpling. Something warm compressed in his chest.

There's my girl.

"There you are, Mr Bone," she said, echoing his thoughts. "I thought perhaps Mr Grey had cornered you with another of his stories, and you might be in need of rescue." The maid closed the distance between them and reached up for a playful tug at his beard, as though she'd done so for years instead of mere days.

"No, I saw to Grey," he said, taking up her hand and heading back towards the hatch. "But the captain wanted a word."

John gave her fingers a squeeze, unfamiliar sentiment welling. He wanted to tell her.

It's too soon John, she'll think you mad.

"Well *I'd* like a word, John Bone," she said, turning to face him at the head of the stair. The galley awaited, below.

"Would you, Brigit O'Creagh?" He mimicked her formality, but curiosity prickled at him.

"Yes," she said, green eyes hopeful, "I've something I need to tell you. Perhaps you'll think I've gone mad …"

WE HOPE YOU ENJOYED *THE MAID AND THE COOK!*

Like what you read?

Why not leave a review on the site where you purchased your copy? Even a short one is always a great help to independent authors, who rely on readers like you to get the word out about their books.

Ready for more?

Sign up for Eris Adderly's email newsletter:
http://eepurl.com/beYqU1

Get notified about upcoming releases, including:

Books 4 and 5 in *The Skull & Crossbone Romances:*

The Carpenter and the Deckhand
The Merry Widow

Eris only sends emails for new releases (both stories for purchase and free reads), no spam. You can unsubscribe at any time and your address will not be shared.

About Eris

Eris writes dark, escape-from-reality romance full of criminals and outcasts. Expect the decadent and filthy, the crude and sublime, sometimes all at once. She is a complete nerd and possible crazy cat lady. She will annoy you with puns.

Also by Eris Adderly

THE SKULL AND CROSSBONE ROMANCES:

The Devil's Luck – Lust and discovery, betrayal and secrets in the age of sail. Oh yes, and pirates. Dirty, dirty pirates. A young widow from Bristol is ready to sail for the Colonies, but fate seems to have other ideas. A full-length erotic bodice-ripper novel to satisfy your thirst for adventure and pleasure on the high seas.

The Decline and Fall of Rowland Graves – A tragic, Gothic romance novella, with a dark, Halloween twist. The origin story of the villainous surgeon who menaced Hannah aboard *The Devil's Luck*.

AFTER EXILE SERIES

BOOK ONE: *An Emperor for the Eclipse* – A man they call 'exile' and a woman they call 'witch' meet their fate on the steps of the imperial palace. Neither will ever be the same. A dark, romantic fantasy.

FLAMES OF OLYMPOS SERIES

BOOK ONE: *The Eighth House: Hades & Persephone* – The Lord of the Dead must take a wife. Persephone is more than he expects. An erotic, BDSM mythological romance.

BLUSHING BOOKS PUBLICATIONS

Gallows Pole – A notorious highway thief makes a dangerous bargain with a hangman in eighteenth century England. A dark, historical erotic romance novella.

Find Eris Online

www.erisadderly.com
www.facebook.com/erisadderly
www.twitter.com/erisadderly

Printed in Great Britain
by Amazon